Jamie lifted a gleaming blue box out of a nest of tissue paper.

On top of the box was a card. "'Happy ninth birthday, Jamie!'" she read aloud. "'I hope you like the enclosed. I bought them from a third-rate wizard who was going out of business. They're supposed to be magic, but don't be disappointed if they don't work. Have fun with them anyway!'"

Jamie laughed. "Trust Great-Aunt Letitia to come up with a crazy story like that."

Inside the box were the greatest sneakers Jamie had ever seen — dazzling pink high-tops with fluorescent green laces. Eagerly Jamie took them out and put them on. They fit perfectly. "You can borrow them if you want, Randy," she said to her friend. "Randy? Why are you looking like that?"

Randy was certainly looking very strange. Her eyes were bulging, her face had turned a deathly white, and her mouth was open in shock.

"Do I have something on my nose? What's going on?" Jamie jumped to her feet and stared at her reflection in the bedroom mirror.

Then she looked again.

And again.

Where her reflection should have been, there was nothing at all.

Jamie had disappeared!

The See-Through Kid

#1
Getting Even
Elissa Snow

PRICE STERN SLOAN
Los Angeles

Produced by Cloverdale Press, Inc.
96 Morton Street
New York, New York 10014

Published by Price Stern Sloan, Inc.
360 North La Cienega Boulevard
Los Angeles, California 90048

ISBN: 0-8431-2722-8

10 9 8 7 6 5 4 3 2 1

Chapter One

"But, Mom, I'm *not* kidding!" Jamie Keenan wailed. "I really think I *do* have pneumonia! Listen to this cough!"

"Okay, I'm listening," her mother said dryly from the doorway.

Jamie was still in bed even though it was already seven o'clock. Of all the thousands of nine-year-old girls who were dreading the thought of starting a new school year, Jamie was probably dreading it the most. She knew that the old "I'm sick" routine was pretty tired, but she couldn't think of any other way to get out of the first day of school.

Jamie cleared her throat and forced out a cough. It sounded like a baby bird learning to chirp. Uh-oh, Jamie thought. I'd better change my tactics. "Too weak even to cough," she said faintly, closing her eyes and sinking back onto her pillow.

Mrs. Keenan strode into the room and yanked the covers off her daughter. "Too weak to convince me, anyway," she said. "I'm afraid you'll live, Jamie. Now get up and get dressed. Betsy made banana-pecan pancakes for breakfast."

1

Betsy was Jamie's sixteen-year-old sister. She was on a diet, so she was always starving. To make herself feel better, Betsy cooked incredible food for the rest of the family to eat. "*Someone* might as well get to eat all the stuff I wish I could have," Betsy always said.

Slowly Jamie climbed out of bed. "Betsy just wants to make the rest of us fat so that she'll look skinny compared to us," she grumbled.

"Well, you certainly don't have to worry about getting fat," her mother said. "Now get going, honey. The school bus will be here in half an hour."

Mrs. Keenan paused at the door. "I did a really nice job with this room," she said thoughtfully. She was an interior decorator, and she'd just finished Jamie's room. It was beautiful — if you liked pink and green. Jamie didn't.

"Okay, see you downstairs," Mrs. Keenan added, walking briskly out the door.

Jamie scowled as she pulled on her jeans. She'd run out of tricks. There was no way she could avoid being on that bus.

This is going to be a horrible year, Jamie thought. I just know it. Why couldn't I have stayed in third grade?

As far as Jamie was concerned, third grade had been okay. But this year Laughing Egg Elementary School had a new principal who was very, very big on physical fitness. Jamie knew this because he'd sent a letter out to all the parents announcing that the school was going to have gym every day from now on.

That means I'm going to feel totally humiliated every day instead of just on Mondays and Thursdays, Jamie brooded. She loved sports — too bad she was completely terrible at all of them. Even her best friend Randy Dowell hesitated before she picked Jamie for a team.

Then there was the problem of Jamie's fourth-grade teacher, Miss Duni. Both of Jamie's older sisters had told her that Miss Duni was a little crazy. And from what Jamie had seen when she passed by Miss Duni's classroom last year, it looked as if her sisters were right.

And as if this weren't bad enough, there was the problem of Bill Baird. He's worse than all my other problems put together, Jamie thought gloomily.

For as long as Jamie had been going to school, Billy Baird — Bill the Pill, as Jamie called him — had been torturing her. In kindergarten he'd told Jamie that her parents turned into witches at night. "I've seen them," he'd said, and a horrified Jamie had believed him. In first grade, he'd cut all the hair off Jamie's Barbie doll. In second grade he'd gotten almost the whole class to call her Mucus-head. In third grade, he'd painted the Keenans' dog pink. Now fourth grade was about to start, and Jamie was absolutely sure Bill would make it his business to be a bigger pill than ever.

Jamie made a face at her reflection in the bedroom mirror. To top it all off, she was really getting tired of the way she looked. What her mother had said was true — she didn't have to worry about getting fat. If anything, she had the opposite problem. Look at my arms! she thought crossly. They're like chicken wings! And my hair's just a big red mop! And those freckles! I am a total mess!

"Gooning at yourself in the mirror again, I see." Margaret's voice intruded on her thoughts. Margaret was her twelve-year-old nightmare of a sister. She never missed a chance to step on Jamie if she could. "Watch out. Your face might break," she giggled.

"Get out of my room!" Jamie yelled, totally irritated by her sister's stupid joke.

"I'm not in your room," Margaret said sweetly. "I'm in the hall. That's why I get to use the bathroom first."

Fifteen minutes later Jamie stamped into the Keenans' breakfast room and plunked herself down in her chair. No one seemed to notice how angry she was. Her father was hidden behind his newspaper, the way he always was before eight-thirty. Her mother was trying to wipe maple syrup and crumbs off her five-year-old brother Tim's face. Margaret was happily digging into a

4

huge stack of pancakes, and Betsy was sipping a glass of water. On her plate was a cup of unsweetened yogurt. She winced every time she took a spoonful of it.

Mr. Keenan lowered the newspaper for a second. "Good morning, Jamie. These pancakes are awfully tasty. I suggest you eat some before they're all gone," he said. Up went the newspaper again.

"I don't want any," Jamie muttered.

"Can I have hers?" Tim asked instantly.

"No, Tim, you may not," answered Mrs. Keenan. "I just cleaned you off. Jamie, honey, you have to eat. You need something in your stomach to do well at school."

"Well, then, I'd rather starve," said Jamie. "Maybe I'll flunk out that way, and I'll be expelled."

Mrs. Keenan set down her coffee cup with a snap. "What is going on with you, young lady?" she asked. "You've always enjoyed going to school until this year. Now fourth grade is about to start, and all of a sudden you've turned into an ogress. Is there a problem you're not telling us about?"

"A problem! Mom, everything about school is going to be a problem this year! I don't even know where to start!"

"If I can't have any more pancakes, then can I have some Rainbow Crunchies?" Tim piped up.

5

"I think that if I go to all this trouble to make the family a nice breakfast, the least Jamie can do is taste it," Betsy complained, her voice trembling.

"Don't get upset, Betsy. You're just weak with hunger, that's all," said Margaret. "Mom, don't let Tim have Rainbow Crunchies. They made him throw up in pastel last time."

"Can't everybody be quiet for one second around here?" Jamie shouted. "I'm trying to talk to Mom!"

Mr. Keenan lowered the sports section. "A little less chaos, everyone," he said mildly before he disappeared again behind his paper.

Margaret didn't pay any attention to her father. "Jamie's got a crush on Bill Baird, Mom," she said excitedly. "And he's in her class this year. That's why she doesn't want to go to school — she's playing hard-to-get." This time both of Jamie's sisters burst into laughter.

Suddenly there was a rumbling sound outside. Jamie glanced up and saw a yellow blur vanishing down the street. "My bus!" she wailed. "I just missed it!"

Mrs. Keenan jumped to her feet. "I'll run out and stop the bus," she said. "You get your stuff and go brush your teeth." She raced out the door, her bedroom slippers flapping loudly with each step. "Wait! Come back! Wait!" she called out.

"Great way to start off the year, Jamie," Betsy said wearily. "The whole neighborhood gets to see Mom in her bathrobe."

"Welcome! Welcome! Welcome to fo-o-o-urth gra-a-a-ade!" Miss Duni sang. She put down her castanets and finished her song with a resounding tattoo on the bongo drums she was holding in her lap. "Yay, class!" she yelled.

Jamie glanced around at the other kids in her new class. To her relief, most of them looked just as shocked and embarrassed as she felt. The two exceptions were Larry Berman and Leesa Alexander. They always loved everything about every teacher and ended up being the teacher's favorites. No one had been expecting that Miss Duni would serenade them with a song she'd written herself.

"Don't worry if you feel a little shy," said Miss Duni. She put down her instruments on her desk and jumped to her feet. Her long, straight hair flew out behind her. "Before the end of the year I just know you'll all be singing along with me."

"Don't count on it," Jamie muttered. From the desk next to hers, Randy shot her a warning glance. Jamie was sure Randy also thought Miss Duni was awful. They usually felt the same way about most things. But Randy got worried when Jamie made a scene.

We're so different it's sometimes hard to believe we're best friends, Jamie mused. Randy dresses up for the first day of school, instead of wearing jeans the way I do. She lives in constant fear of getting into trouble. She looks on the bright side of things. She's always polite. And I . . .

Bill Baird's grating voice instantly brought Jamie back to the classroom. "Jamie Keenan's a good singer, Miss Duni," said Bill brightly from his seat right behind Jamie. "I've heard her sing many a gay tune." The class erupted into giggles.

Miss Duni didn't seem to notice the giggles. She gave Jamie a warm smile. "That's wonderful, Jamie," she said. Then her expression became serious. "Now, class, I know we will all be friends. I don't want you to think of me as just another teacher. I have lots of fun ideas, you know. Here's an example of one of them."

Miss Duni reached into one of her desk drawers and pulled out some cards. "Take a look at this," she said proudly. She began passing around a large, square piece of cardboard with insects pinned onto it.

There was a murmur of astonishment from the class as the piece of cardboard was circulated around the room. "But this is just a bunch of old dead bugs!" Bill said loudly.

Jamie saw that he was right. Dozens of dead insects pinned in neat rows wasn't only uninteresting — it was gross. Jamie absolutely hated bugs, dead or alive. Shuddering, she prayed she would disappear into thin air before the bug board reached her.

"Not dead bugs, Bill," corrected Miss Duni in a solemn voice. "*Insect specimens.* And this is just the beginning."

Miss Duni's eyes were glowing behind her round glasses. "You know, class," she said, "every fourth grade in our school will be studying insects this year. But only our class will be having regular Bug Sessions."

The class stared blankly at her.

"We're going to *immerse* ourselves in insect life — lose ourselves in the world of bugs," said Miss Duni. "For six glorious weeks we'll learn *everything* about insects. By the end of that time, I hope we'll understand them so well we'll all feel like insects."

"That shouldn't be hard for you, Keenan," Bill whispered under his breath.

"Now, we're all going to be working in pairs," Miss Duni continued. "Next week each pair will be assigned one particular insect to study. I'll be assigning the insects then. But I prepared the list of partners last night." With a flourish she pulled a piece of paper off her desk. "Here it is."

Jamie and Randy looked hopefully at each other. If only Randy and I could be partners, Jamie thought, Bug Sessions wouldn't be that disgusting after all!

"Mike Liu and Wendy Shapiro," read Miss Duni. "Judy Gollin and Todd Dorsett." Uh-oh, Jamie thought. She's made boy-girl teams! "Cammy Wright and Jim Martinelli. Randy Dowell and Larry Berman," Miss Duni went on. Randy sighed in disappointment, but she did it so quietly that only Jamie heard her.

"Jamie Keenan and Bill Baird."

Jamie couldn't believe what she'd just heard. "Could you repeat that, Miss Duni?" she asked faintly.

"Jamie Keenan and Bill Baird," the teacher repeated.

With a groan, Jamie slid down in her chair. Bill the Pill is my partner for Bug Sessions! How am I going to stand six weeks of Bill Baird and bugs?

"What are you groaning about, Jamie?" Bill said loudly. "I think it'll be fun working together!"

"That's the spirit, Bill!" said Miss Duni. She placed the list back on her desk.

And at that moment Jamie felt Bill's hand tugging at the back of her collar. She whipped around to face him — and realized that he was just about to drop a huge dead beetle down her back.

The second he saw her horrified expression, he did.

Chapter Two

"I just hope my mother doesn't ask me how my day went," Jamie said to Randy a few hours later as the two girls walked home from school together. "Because if I told her the truth, she'd probably faint."

"Things have got to be better tomorrow, anyway," said Randy reassuringly.

But Jamie wasn't so sure.

Mrs. Keenan was reading to Tim in the living room when Jamie and Randy walked through the front door. "Hi, girls," she said. "I just made some chocolate-chip cookies — they're on the kitchen counter. And there's a package for you on the kitchen table, Jamie."

"Hey, it's from Great-Aunt Letitia!" Jamie said when she saw the spidery writing on the label. "Boy, it's about time something good happened today. Let's take our cookies to my room. I want to open this without Tim spying on me."

"Who's Great-Aunt Letitia?" asked Randy, grabbing a handful of cookies as they walked down the hall to Jamie's room.

"Oh, she's my father's mother's sister." Jamie plunked herself down on her ruffled bedspread and struggled to undo the cord tied around the package. "She lives in Philadelphia. Hand me those scissors on my desk, will you? She's really old, and she's a little crazy, but she always gives great presents — the kind you don't ask for because you never knew they existed. When I was little she gave me a bears' dollhouse carved out of a hollow log, with moss rugs and acorn-cap plates, and once she gave Betsy a whole perfume-making kit. . . . There we go." Jamie lifted a gleaming blue box out of a nest of tissue paper.

On top of the box was a card. "'Happy ninth birthday, Jamie!'" Jamie read aloud. Actually, her birthday had been three months ago. Great-Aunt Letitia tended to forget when Jamie's birthday was, though she seemed to have no trouble remembering the exact date of the other Keenan birthdays. "'I hope you like the enclosed,'" Jamie continued. "'I bought them from a third-rate wizard who was going out of business. They're supposed to be magic, but don't be disappointed if they don't work. Have fun with them anyway!'"

Jamie laughed. "Trust Great-Aunt Letitia to come up with a crazy story like that. Hey, look!"

Inside the box were the greatest sneakers Jamie had ever seen. They were high-tops — she'd been wanting a pair for months — a dazzling bright pink pair with fluorescent green laces.

"I can't believe an old lady would buy you such a cool present!" Randy marveled. "My own mother would never let me have high-tops!"

"I told you — Great-Aunt Letitia always knows what we want. I don't even care that she's three months late!" Eagerly Jamie lifted the sneakers out and put them on. They fit her perfectly. "Oh, I can't wait for Margaret to see these," she said. "She'll be so jealous. You can borrow them if you want, though, Randy. Randy? Why are you looking at me like that? Randy?" Jamie repeated, staring at her silent friend.

Randy was certainly looking very strange. More than strange — she seemed to have frozen in place. Her eyes were bulging, her face had turned a deathly white, and her mouth was open in shock as she stared at Jamie.

"Do I have something on my nose? What's going on? Say something, Ran!"

Randy's mouth opened a little wider, but no sound came out.

"It can't be *that* bad," Jamie said, getting just a little bit concerned now. "Can it?" She jumped to her feet and stared at her reflection in the bedroom mirror.

Then she looked again. And again.

She could see the reflection of her bed piled with stuffed animals. She could see Randy — whose shocked face was now definitely green — and her desk and her lamp and the curtains at the window.

What Jamie didn't see was herself. Where her reflection should have been, there was nothing at all.

Jamie had disappeared! For a whole minute the room was silent. "Wh-what happened to me? Where am I?" Jamie asked, her voice quivering.

Randy was still staring at the place where Jamie should have been. "I don't know," she said in a whisper. "But that wizard must have known more about magic than your aunt thought."

Jamie stuck both arms straight out in front of her. This morning she'd been mad because they looked like chicken wings. Now she'd have been glad to see them even if they were covered with feathers. But there were no arms to be seen.

She crossed her eyes, trying desperately to stare down at the nose she usually hated because it looked like a skijump. But there was no nose to look at. Even her brand-new sneakers were gone.

"I want to go home," Randy said, sounding like she was about to start crying.

"No!" Jamie said, panic-stricken. "Don't leave me here, wherever I am! What if I've — I've dissolved or something?"

"You can't have dissolved. You wouldn't be able to talk!" said Randy.

"But how do I know for sure that I'm still here?"

"Try pinching yourself," Randy suggested.

Jamie grabbed a fold of skin on the back of her left hand and squeezed it as hard as she could. "Ow!" she yelped. "I guess I must still be here. I guess . . . I must be *invisible,* Ran! These sneakers really *are* magic!"

There was a knock at the door. "Jamie?" Mrs. Keenan called.

"*No,* Mom!" Jamie said frantically. She sat down on the edge of her bed and began wrenching off her new high-tops as fast as she could. "Don't come in! I'm right in here, just the way I always am!"

"That's right, Mrs. Keenan!" called Randy. "We're both in here as plain as the nose on your face!"

There was a little pause from the other side of the door. "Of course you are," Mrs. Keenan finally said. "I never doubted that. I just wanted to tell you I'm leaving your folded laundry outside the door, Jamie. Be sure to put it away, will you?"

"Yes, Mom!" Jamie got the second sneaker off just as she spoke — and the minute it was off she was visible again.

For a second she and Randy stared at each other. Then Jamie whooped excitedly. "Can you believe this?" she yelled.

16

Randy looked just as excited as Jamie felt. "Put them back on," she begged. "I want to see it happen again."

Jamie did as Randy asked. This time she watched herself in the mirror as she laced up the sneakers. The instant the second lace was tied, her reflection disappeared again. It was like being erased.

Randy grinned incredulously as Jamie vanished.

"Boy, I'd better remember to write Great-Aunt Letitia a thank-you note," Jamie said. "Let's try going outside!"

"You mean, with you invisible like that?" Randy asked.

"Of course!" Jamie said. "I've got to try out my new powers! We can go to the park for a little while before supper. Just tell my mother you have to go home now when you walk by her — I can hear her down in the kitchen. I'll be right behind you."

"I have to go home now, Mrs. Keenan," Randy said in an artificially bright voice a couple of minutes later. Randy had never been very good at lying. "Time to hit the books, you know!"

"See you soon, Randy," said Mrs. Keenan.

"See you soon, Randy," Randy repeated nervously. "I mean, see you soon, Mrs. Keenan. Jamie's upstairs, by the way. Doing her homework, you know what I mean? Okay, 'bye!"

"Why'd you tell her that about me?" Jamie hissed as the two of them walked down the driveway. "Of course she'd assume I was upstairs! Now what happens if she tries to find me?"

"I was afraid she'd ask where you were!" Randy wailed. "I'm sorry, Jamie. It's going to take a little while before I get used to all this."

A little boy eyed Randy curiously as he passed by. "Who are you talking to?" he called back over his shoulder.

"Oh!" Randy's face was pink. "I didn't think that would happen! Jamie, for heaven's sake, don't talk to me until we're alone."

Without saying another word, the girls headed down the street and took the turn that led to the park two blocks from Jamie's house. At the park's entrance they passed a woman walking her dog. She smiled politely at Randy.

"I'm all by myself, you know," said Randy awkwardly.

"*Randy!*" Jamie hissed under her breath. She grabbed Randy's arm and yanked her away from the entrance. "Oh, good," she said with relief. "There's no one at the playground."

The playground stood deserted in the late-afternoon sun. So no one noticed when Randy began swinging — and the empty swing next to her began swinging, too.

"Just imagine all the stuff I'll be able to do now!" Jamie said.

18

"I know," Randy answered dreamily. "It's — it's almost like being an angel or something. You could do secret good deeds for people. Say there's this poor old lady who's living in a little hut or something, and she's too proud to let anyone help her. Every day you could put on your high-tops and sneak over with a basket of delicious food for her — I could help you put together the basket and you could clean up her hut while she's sleeping. You'd have to be really quiet, of course. Why, she'd think a good fairy had been there —"

"Well, the basket-of-food part doesn't sound too bad, but I'm not sure I want to use my enchanted sneakers to clean up someone's hut," Jamie interrupted. "I think I'll wait on the good deeds for a while, Ran. I want to have a . . . uh-oh, wait a minute! Someone's coming!"

A tired-looking girl who looked about fourteen or fifteen was walking into the park holding the hand of a plump, snub-nosed little girl with blond ringlets. Even at a distance, Jamie and Randy could hear the little girl's shrill voice.

"But, Claire, you're just my *baby-sitter,* not my mother. So you *have* to let me do what I want!" she was screaming. "You have to let me go on the swings! You have to! You —"

"Okay, Larissa," said the baby-sitter exhaustedly. "But just for a few minutes. You know your mother said to come straight home."

19

"Good," said Larissa smugly. "Now, make that stupid girl over there stop swinging. I want to swing all by myself." Her mean little eyes glared at Randy.

Claire looked at Randy with an embarrassed shrug. "Make her get off!" screeched Larissa.

"I take it back, Randy," Jamie said under her breath. "I think my first good deed's just about to happen. I'm going to help Little Miss Pig swing."

"Good idea," Randy murmured. "I'll help." She jumped off the swing and beamed at Larissa.

"Would you like a push, honey?" she asked.

"No. Just get out of the way," Larissa answered, tossing her patent-leather purse at the baby-sitter's feet. She marched toward the swings, clambered aboard, and began pumping vigorously. Her fat little legs dangled in the air.

Without thinking, Jamie jumped off her own swing when it was still much too high. To her amazement, she landed on her feet as gracefully as a cat. Maybe these sneakers do more than make me invisible! she thought. Maybe they make me less klutzy, too!

She positioned herself behind Larissa and began pushing with all her strength. The swing swooped crazily through the air. Holding on for dear life, Larissa lurched backward and forward along with it.

"Good pumping, honey!" Randy said encouragingly.

"Claire!" Larissa shrieked. "Stop it! I want to get off!"

Abruptly Jamie grabbed the seat of the swing. Larissa tumbled off and landed facedown in the dirt.

Jamie knelt down next to her. "This is your conscience speaking," she said in a voice too low for anyone else to hear. "Next time, don't be such a pig to your nice baby-sitter."

Astonished, Larissa sat up and brushed the dirt off her face. "Now apologize to Claire for being so obnoxious," Jamie continued quietly.

"I — I'm sorry I was rude, Claire," Larissa faltered.

Claire looked even more amazed by the apology than she had by what had happened to Larissa on the swing. "That's okay," she said. "Let's get home now." Hand in hand, Claire and Larissa left the playground.

"Where's your hand?" said Randy. "I want to shake it. That was great, Jamie."

Jamie grinned. "Just call me the Invisible Avenger," she answered. "Ran, I can't see my watch, but I think I'd better get home before my supper disappears, too. Call me tonight, okay?"

Jamie ran all the way home. It really did seem as though the sneakers made her more athletic. Who knew what else they could do?

It sure is fun to do your homework when you're invisible, Jamie thought as she watched her pencil skip magically across the page. Even though I'm not any better at arithmetic than I was in third grade.

Jamie had slipped the sneakers off just before supper, a meal she could hardly remember eating now. Betsy had made the family a huge platter of fried chicken and dumplings (and a broiled drumstick for herself), but Jamie had been too excited to know what she was eating. For the first time in her life she'd even skipped dessert. All she wanted to do was to get upstairs and try out her high-tops again.

The sneakers were back on now. Jamie was trying to add some fractions when the phone rang. "Jamie, it's for you," her father called.

"Thanks! I'll take it in here!" Jamie called back. Thank heaven I got my own phone for my birthday, she thought. "Hello?"

"Hi, it's Randy."

"Hi, Ran! Boy, I hope you can help me with this math. You're a lot better at it than I am."

"Sure, I'll help," said Randy. "But I was really calling to ask if you want to go shopping tomorrow after school."

Jamie sighed. "Randy, after all these years you should know I hate shopping. All I ever seem to do is stand around and watch you try on clothes. Then you call your mom and ask if you

22

can buy whatever you've just tried on, and she says no. You get disappointed, and we bike home. Is that any way to spend an afternoon?"

"But you could bring your sneakers!"

There was a little pause. "Yes, that does make shopping sound a lot more interesting," Jamie finally said. "Sure, Ran. We can —"

"Jamie, can I come in?"

Jamie froze. It was her brother Tim. And, as always, he barged into the room without waiting for her answer.

"Jamie?" he said.

"Jamie?" came Randy's tiny voice out of the phone receiver. "Are you there?"

Tim turned and stared in Jamie's direction. Jamie realized that the phone receiver she was holding must look as though it were floating in midair.

"What's going on, Jamie?" Randy squeaked.

Tim's eyes were round with astonishment.

As slowly as possible, Jamie inched the receiver down to the desk top and hung it up. *Sorry, Randy,* she apologized silently to her friend. *I'll call you back.* The phone rang almost instantly. Jamie tensed in her chair. "Jamie, it's for you!" Betsy called.

"She's not in here!" shouted Tim. "She got sucked into the phone. She's trapped!"

"Oh, Tim!" Jamie heard Betsy say crossly. "You and your imagination. I'll tell Randy to call back later."

Jamie relaxed a little. But she could see that Tim would not be put off so easily. He reached out a cautious finger and poked the phone receiver. When it didn't do anything, he picked it up and stared at it.

"Jamie?" he whispered. "Are you in there?"

Then he noticed the pencil on the desk where Jamie had left it. His eyes brightened, and Jamie could tell he'd forgotten about her for the moment.

He picked up the pencil to draw some pictures and plunked himself down at the desk — on Jamie's lap.

Jamie gasped, and Tim leaped to his feet as if he'd been scalded. "Dad!" he shrieked. "There's a — a phone monster in Jamie's room! First it ate Jamie, and then I sat on it!"

"Now, Tim, stop fooling around and get in here for your bath," Mr. Keenan called.

"But, Dad, Jamie's inside the phone!"

"Tim, I'm getting tired of your stalling. You know you have to take a bath tonight. Now get in here!" called their father.

"But what about *Jamie?*" Tim bellowed.

"Timothy Keenan! Do I have to count to three?"

Tim gulped. "No, Dad," he called back. He turned to Jamie's chair — which of course appeared to be empty. "I'll get you, monster," he said. He picked up Jamie's dictionary and whacked it down hard on the telephone.

The dictionary bounced off the desk and crashed onto Jamie's kneecaps. It took all her strength not to scream.

"You give Jamie back!" Tim hollered at the phone.

"Coming, Dad!" He dashed off to the bathroom.

Alone again, Jamie cautiously rubbed her throbbing knees. I guess I'd better not be invisible when people are home, she thought. It's too risky.

But everywhere else . . .

Jamie smiled. For the first time in days she was in a good mood again. A pair of magic high-tops made life look a whole lot different.

Now she'd be able to go to all sorts of places she couldn't before. She'd be able to find out what people really thought of her. She'd be able to play sports without making a fool of herself.

And maybe, just maybe, she'd be able to get even with Bill the Pill Baird.

Chapter Three

"Have a good time at the mall!" Margaret called as Jamie and Randy climbed onto their bikes. "If you see Billy Baird, give him a big kiss!"

"Someday I'm going to kill Margaret," said Jamie between clenched teeth.

"Forget it," Randy said. "Let's plan what we're going to do now instead."

School had just let out, and Jamie and Randy were heading toward the mall near Jamie's house. Jamie had brought her magic sneakers with her, but she wasn't wearing them yet. She didn't think Randy was up to explaining why the bike next to her had no rider.

After last night's phone fiasco, Jamie decided that she and Randy needed to set up ground rules for how to deal with Jamie's new powers. "Ran, if I suddenly hang up the phone, you'll know from now on that something is wrong," Jamie explained. "Also, you have to cover for me when I disappear."

"Well, I'll try to, anyway," Randy said. "Just promise me that you won't disappear in front of people more than you have to. And, Jamie," she

26

added solemnly, "I want you to promise me one thing — that you'll never, ever use your new sneakers to cheat or steal."

"Of course I won't!" said Jamie.

"Good," said Randy. She sounded relieved.

"You know, Ran, wouldn't you like to borrow the sneakers sometime soon? I'd be happy to cover for you," Jamie offered.

But Randy looked horrified. "I just couldn't! What if I got into trouble or something? No, Jamie, you keep them. But thanks," she added.

They reached the mall and parked at a bike rack behind one of the stores. Then Randy stood guard while Jamie crawled behind a bush, took off the old white sneakers she'd been wearing, and put on her pink high-tops.

Nothing happened.

"I'm still here!" Jamie said blankly.

"Maybe you didn't tie the laces tight enough," Randy suggested.

Jamie tightened them, but she stayed as visible as ever.

"Great! They only worked for one day!" she said in disgust. "Well, there go all my plans. Thanks a lot, Great-Aunt Letitia." She stared glumly down at her feet.

"At least we had fun yesterday!" Randy chirped.

Jamie didn't answer. She hated it when anyone — even her best friend — tried to cheer her up.

"Oh, come on, Jamie," Randy coaxed her. "We're here. We might as well do something. Let's go to Monroe's first." Monroe's was Randy's favorite department store. "Maybe trying on clothes will cheer you up."

"Okay," Jamie said listlessly, dragging herself to her feet.

At the entrance to Monroe's, Jamie accidentally bumped into a rather large woman in a mink coat. "Oops! Sorry," she said. "I guess I wasn't paying attention to where I was going."

"I guess not, young lady!" the woman trumpeted. She clutched her purse tightly and glared at Jamie. "Really, I don't know what children are coming to these days. Running through the streets like hooligans, grabbing whatever they can get their little hands on —"

"Have a nice day, ma'am!" Randy interrupted. She put a firm hand on Jamie's arm and steered her away. "Don't pay any attention," she said. "That kind of person is just looking for a fight. Now, what do you want to try on first?"

"Why don't you go try on some stuff, and I'll meet you in an hour," Jamie said. "I'm still so mad about these dumb sneakers that I wouldn't be much fun anyway. Go on, Ran," she added when Randy hesitated. "I'll find stuff to do."

"Okay," Randy said. "I'll see you in the Junior Jeans department in an hour."

Now, what can I do to cheer myself up? Jamie wondered as she walked aimlessly along.

"Would you like to try our newest perfume?" asked a woman holding a basket of crystal bottles. "It's called Dream of Love. Here, let me spray some on you —"

"No, thanks! No, thanks!" Jamie said quickly, veering out of the woman's way.

As the perfume lady strolled away, Jamie stopped to get her bearings. She realized that she was in the Better Dresses department, a place she'd never paid any attention to before. Evening gowns were the kind of thing Randy liked. But today the haughty-looking mannequin which stood in the center of the department was wearing one of the most beautiful gowns Jamie had ever seen. It was black satin covered with tiny silver stars, and it had a huge black velvet bow in back.

Jamie stroked the shiny fabric longingly. Boy, this would make a great Halloween costume, she thought. If I got a hat, I could be a fairy godmother or —

"May I help you?" came a sharp voice behind her.

Startled, Jamie turned around. A plump saleswoman with a beaky nose and a gray bun was glaring at her. Her name tag read "Miss Rose."

"C-can I try this on?" Jamie stammered. She wondered how such an ugly woman could have such a pretty name.

"I think you mean 'may I.' You certainly may not," said Miss Rose. Her eyes swept disdainfully over Jamie's jeans, sweatshirt, and sneakers. "This dress costs thousands of dollars. We can't have little girls wandering in and ruining — "

At that moment Jamie turned invisible.

"What?" Miss Rose squawked. "Where did she go?"

The sneakers still worked! Maybe not right away, but the magic was still in there somewhere! Jamie shook a triumphant fist at the ceiling.

Miss Rose rubbed her eyes. "She must have run away," she muttered. "I'll make sure to report her."

See you later, Miss Rose, Jamie thought happily. She'd just noticed the fat woman in the fur coat heading toward the wig department.

Of course Monroe's didn't call it the wig department. They called it Hair With Flair. And the fur lady's real hair didn't have much flair at all, Jamie noticed as the woman took her hat off. It looked like a pile of gray straw.

"I would like to see something in an auburn shade," she told the saleswoman. "That one there looks just right." She pointed to a wig made of long, bright red ringlets.

"Madame, if I might suggest something more . . . uh . . . dignified? That wig is a trifle frivolous, perhaps?" the saleswoman said nervously.

"Are you saying I'm too old for this wig?" the lady snapped.

"No, no! But we do want madame to look her best, do we not? Now this would be perfect for madame." The saleswoman held up a plain gray wig.

"Stop trying to make me look old! And stop breathing down my neck!"

"I beg your pardon, madame?"

Jamie was the one doing the breathing, of course. She had crept right up behind the fur lady. The Invisible Avenger is about to strike again, Jamie thought.

"Forget it," said the fur lady. "Just hand me that auburn wig, please."

Silently the saleswoman handed the pile of red ringlets to the woman, who put it on. It looked exactly like clown's hair. From the way she was trying to hide a smile, you could tell that the saleswoman thought so, too.

Jamie reached out and gave the wig a little yank. It slithered off the lady's head and landed on the floor in a tangled heap.

"This thing won't even stay on!" the fur lady complained. She picked the wig up and jammed it on her head again — and again Jamie tugged it off.

"Perhaps madame's natural hair is slippery," suggested the saleswoman. "Maybe a touch of wig adhesive would do the trick." She took out a tube and smeared some glop around the inside edges of the wig. "Let's try again," she said.

The wig looked a little crooked, but it stayed on. That was because Jamie didn't touch it this time. The fur lady looked ridiculous — but she obviously liked what she saw in the mirror. "You see?" she told the saleswoman gaily. "I was right. It's extremely attractive on me. I'll take it."

And Jamie let the fur lady keep the wig on until the unsuspecting woman had sat down and ordered lunch in Monroe's restaurant. Then Jamie pulled the monstrosity off and dumped it — glue, hair and all — into the fur lady's fruit-and-cottage-cheese platter.

Jamie didn't stick around to watch what happened next. She still wanted to try on that evening gown, and there wasn't much time left before she had to meet Randy. She headed back down the escalator toward Better Dresses.

Of course Jamie couldn't resist stopping a few times along the way. She had to make a mannequin wave at startled customers in the menswear department, and she had to sample a few of the delicacies in the bakery — and she had to switch the channels on the TVs in the electronics department, just to see what the people watching them would do. (Much to her disappointment, they didn't do anything. They just kept watching.)

But at last Jamie reached Better Dresses. The black dress looked more beautiful than ever — and Miss Rose was nowhere to be seen.

Jamie looked around, wondering if Miss Rose was at lunch. No one was watching. Carefully she lifted the mannequin wearing the black dress off its pedestal. Then she carried it into one of the fitting rooms.

Wow! Jamie thought, looking around. The fitting rooms in Better Dresses are certainly a lot nicer than the ones in Teens for Today!

The Teens for Today fitting rooms had nothing in them but posters warning shoplifters that hidden cameras were spying on them from behind the mirrors. But each fitting room in Better Dresses had pink wallpaper, a three-way mirror, and a little couch.

Jamie laid the mannequin on the couch and carefully took the dress off the dummy. Then she turned to the mirror and slipped the gown on. As soon as she pulled the dress over her head, it became as invisible as she was.

Well, maybe it's better this way, Jamie thought. Now I can wear it as long as I want!

Even though she couldn't see the dress, it felt wonderful. I'm like Cinderella! Jamie marveled. Who would have thought that a dress could make such a difference in how I feel?

She turned to look at the bare mannequin on the sofa before she swept out of the fitting room.

33

Then she turned around again. Maybe I should put the mannequin back, she thought. Then Miss Rose will freak out when she sees that the dress is gone.

Jamie picked up the mannequin and carried it back out to the pedestal. She stood it up and tried to arrange it in the same pose as before.

Suddenly Jamie became visible again.

And suddenly Miss Rose returned, carrying a cup of coffee. "Why," Miss Rose whooped, "you nasty little girl!"

There was only one thing to do — run. Jamie headed out of the department at full speed.

Unfortunately, she wasn't used to running in dresses that were longer than she was. She'd taken only two steps before she tripped over the hem of the black gown and sprawled on the floor. Miss Rose thudded down on top of her like a huge bag of cement.

"*Ooof!*" Jamie grunted. Somehow she managed to scramble to her feet and get as far as the perfume counter before she tripped again. It was just bad luck that she bumped into the Dream of Love woman, who dropped her basket full of bottles.

A horrible, sickly-sweet scent filled the air. Coughing and choking, Jamie stumbled to her feet again and lurched toward the Junior Jeans department where she was supposed to meet Randy.

If only Randy's there on time, she thought wildly, then she can help me come up with an explanation for all this.

But that was before she crashed into a man who'd just bought eight porcelain figurines.

As Jamie stared, appalled, at all the damage she'd done, she felt two fingers close like steel pincers around her right ear.

"I think it's time I called a security guard," said Miss Rose.

"I don't want to hear any more about it, Jamie," said Mrs. Keenan sharply.

"But, Mom, I wasn't doing anything wrong! You're allowed to try on clothes in a department store!"

"Trying on clothes is one thing. Trying on a four-thousand-dollar evening gown is another. And taking it off the mannequin! And breaking everything within a two-mile radius! Jamie, what in the world got into you?"

"I'm not going to punish you, Jamie," said Mrs. Keenan. "I think you've embarrassed yourself enough already. But don't ever, ever make me go through this again, okay?"

"I promise," Jamie said sincerely. "Thanks, Mom."

Alone in her bedroom, she sat down to think. It was clear that the sneakers weren't going to work the same way every time. Yesterday the magic began when she put them on and ended when she took them off. Today, the magic was far less predictable, as if the sneakers had a mind of their own. . . .

Maybe I shouldn't take so many risks with these sneakers, Jamie thought. Maybe I — Suddenly Margaret poked her face in the door. She was grinning from ear to ear. Betsy was standing right behind her, looking upset.

"We heard about your little adventure, Jamie," said Margaret. "Sounds like fun. Did you try on any wedding dresses while you were at it? You know, I think the name Mrs. Bill Baird is just about the sweetest thing I've ever heard."

"It's not really all that funny," said Betsy plaintively. "I always shop at Monroe's. Now I'll feel humiliated every time I go in there. Why do you have to act like such a baby, Jamie?"

"Get out of here, both of you!" Jamie snapped.

"We're not actually in your room," Margaret reminded her.

Jamie pounded her desk top in rage, got up, and slammed her door shut. I hate them! she fumed. They'd better watch out, because I'm going to get them — especially Margaret!

No, not me, Jamie corrected herself. The Invisible Avenger is going to get them!

Chapter Four

"What are you doing today, Margaret?" asked Jamie at Sunday breakfast three days later.

"*I'm* going fishing," said Tim loudly, to no one in particular.

Margaret eyed Jamie suspiciously. "A bunch of my friends are coming over," she answered. "Why? You weren't planning on joining us, were you?"

"I wouldn't dream of it," said Jamie. "I just wondered. What about you, Betsy?"

Betsy put down the head of lettuce she was halfheartedly gnawing. "Jamie, what do you have up your sleeve?" she asked. "Usually you couldn't care less what we do."

"Nothing!" said Jamie. "Can't a person ask about her own sisters once in a while out of sheer love?"

"A person can, but you never do," said Betsy. "Well, if you really want to know, I'm going out with Steve tonight." Steve was Betsy's boyfriend. Jamie was certain he was the most boring person on earth. "Is that okay with you?"

"Me? Sure," said Jamie innocently. "Have fun!"

Margaret and Betsy didn't realize that *Jamie* was the one who was planning to have fun — the Invisible Avenger was about to strike.

Two hours later, when six girls arrived and trooped upstairs to Margaret's room, Jamie was right behind them.

It was the first time in ages she'd been in Margaret's room. Margaret always kept the door firmly shut, especially when her friends were over. Sometimes Jamie snuck in while Margaret was out, but she was always too nervous to do any real snooping.

Jamie cast an envious look around Margaret's room. Why didn't I get the red-and-white room? she wondered. Why did Mom decide that green and pink were my colors? Look at all the great stuff she put in here — everything Margaret asked for! A window seat, built-in bookcases, and not a ruffle in sight!

Jamie sighed. Mom's too proud of these rooms for me to say anything, she thought. Maybe when I'm twelve she'll let me have a room I really like.

The girls settled down in chairs and on Margaret's twin beds while Jamie did a quick inspection of Margaret's bureau. It was disappointingly ordinary — a brush and comb, some breath spray, five kinds of unused lipstick. . . .

Hey! Jamie thought suddenly. What's this?

It was a scrap of paper. On it Margaret had written her name over and over again. She'd used a different name each time:

Margaret J. Hopkins

Mrs. Tony Hopkins

Mr. and Mrs. Anthony Hopkins

Margaret Keenan-Hopkins

Dr. Meg Keenan and Anthony Hopkins, Esq.

MKH

Tony Hopkins! Jamie couldn't believe it. Tony was a red-faced, hulking fourteen-year-old who lived down the street. Once or twice he'd shoveled the driveway for the Keenans, but Margaret had never so much as mentioned his name.

The next time she teases me about Bill the Pill, thought Jamie, I'm really going to let her have it. I'll keep this piece of paper as evidence. Jamie slipped the scrap of paper into her jeans pocket — where it also became invisible. Then she settled back against the wall to see what Margaret and her friends talked about in private, ready to hear some great secrets.

"So have you guys finished that history chapter yet?" Margaret asked.

There were sighs from around the room. "It's so long," groaned Margaret's friend, Tina. "I'll never finish it by Monday! Mr. Sherbinski is such a slave driver."

Enough already, thought Jamie impatiently. Get to the interesting stuff!

"Anyone rented any good movies lately?"

"I am getting so fat."

"I can't believe how early my mother makes me go to bed."

"Who wants some gum? It's sugarless."

Jamie couldn't believe it — this was getting worse and worse. Margaret kept her door shut for this?

I'm wasting my time here, she told herself. Cautiously she stood up and began tiptoeing toward the door. Maybe she could turn the handle very, very gradually, and then slowly open . . .

"Where's Jamie, Margaret? You'd think she'd have started pestering us by now," said Tiffany Dibble, Margaret's oldest friend.

Jamie stopped in her tracks. This was definitely worth hearing.

"Oh, I don't know," said Margaret wearily. "She's been such a pain lately. All she does is complain about school and Bill Baird."

"Bill Baird? Is he Nancy's little brother?" asked Gem Frothingham.

"That's the one," said Margaret.

"Well, I can understand why Jamie would complain about him," put in Evie Munter. "He's a disgusting slime mold. There is *nothing* to like about him. Nancy's the same way."

"I know, I know," said Margaret. "But it gets so boring around here — there's nothing to do but tease her about him, and watch her throw a

41

fit. Now that's fun! And all my parents do is say I have to be more understanding. Hey, I'm the preteen around here! I'm the one who needs understanding! But you know how parents are. They always let their youngest kids get away with murder."

Jamie's face turned an invisible shade of scarlet. Did Margaret really think she could get away with teasing her for fun?

"Still, she's not so bad," said Gem Frothingham.

"Yeah, but little kids in general drive me crazy," said Margaret.

"*Little!*" exclaimed Jamie aloud. Then she froze, petrified with horror.

There was a sudden silence in the room. "Jamie?" Margaret said grimly. "You can come out now, wherever you are."

"I *knew* someone was in here!" exclaimed Julie Esner with a shudder. "I could just feel it!

"Yeah, but she's not in here," Tiffany said practically. "I mean, she's not under the bed, and she's not in the closet, so — "

"She must be in the hall," Margaret said grimly. She stood up, walked to the door and wrenched it open.

That was Jamie's cue. She darted under Margaret's arm and ran on tiptoes to her own room.

"There's no one out here, either," she heard Margaret say in a bewildered voice. "But I'll *still* kill her when I find her."

His razor-sharp claws dripping blood, the monster lurched toward the screaming nine-year-old girl who was about to become his next victim. She ran with all her might, but clearly she was growing weak. Suddenly she tripped over a tree root and plummeted to the ground. The monster leaned forward, claws outstretched . . .

"Boy, this is a great movie," said Betsy's boyfriend Steve contentedly.

Jamie had learned her lesson from what had happened with Margaret. No more eavesdropping! But that didn't mean she couldn't use her sneakers to be an invisible chaperone.

Jamie hadn't known that Betsy and Steve were planning to see *Fresh Graves, Part IV.* Jamie was sitting next to Betsy. The theater was packed. Every member of the audience except Steve was about to die of terror, but Jamie was pretty sure she felt the worst. At home she couldn't watch horror movies unless her parents were in the room with her and she had a coat over her head. (She peeked out through the buttonholes.)

Fresh Graves was the scariest movie she'd ever seen. But Jamie couldn't use a coat without

43

calling too much attention to herself. And she couldn't keep her eyes closed, either. She was too afraid something with razor-sharp claws would ooze up beside her and grab her.

With a supreme effort, the girl on the screen wrenched herself out of the monster's grip. Stumbling, and half fainting, she began to run again. There was a garage up ahead of her. She dashed through its open door — and into the arms of another monster who was waiting for her inside.

"*Aaaaaaaaaaaaaaaaaahhhhhhh!*"Jamie shrieked.

Everyone in the theater turned around.

"Betsy? Was that you?" asked Steve.

"N-no," Betsy answered. "I thought it was you!"

"Must've been you, honey," the man on Jamie's other side said to Betsy. "It sure wasn't me. Lots of times, you know, people scream without even realizing it. It's a medical fact."

"Oh, it is not," said Betsy. "Anyway, I didn't scream. I could see that scene coming a mile away."

That made Jamie feel even worse. Not only had she embarrassed herself in front of a whole movie theater, but she hadn't been able to foresee the second monster.

"Quiet back there!" someone yelled from the front row. "We're trying to watch a movie here!"

44

Jamie clenched her fists. There was still another hour of *Fresh Graves* left. And she had to stay and watch it. Steve and Betsy were her only way of getting home.

"Well, don't you worry, honey," Steve murmured soothingly to Betsy, "because ol' Steve's here to protect you." He leaned over to kiss Betsy.

"Oh, no," Jamie groaned.

"Quiet!" the man in the front row hollered again.

Steve straightened up. "What's the matter?" he asked in a worried voice.

"Nothing," said Betsy. "Why would anything be the matter?"

"That's what I asked you. Don't you want to kiss me?" Steve said in an undertone.

"Of course I do! What are you talking about?" Betsy whispered back.

Looking relieved, Steve bent to kiss Betsy again.

I am going to barf right here if he doesn't stop it, thought Jamie. She reached over Betsy's shoulder and pushed Steve's face away.

He straightened up again, and this time he looked offended. "Betsy, if you're mad at me, just say so!" he whispered urgently.

"Steve, what is going on?" said Betsy, forgetting to talk quietly.

"*Shut up!* " shouted the man in the front row.

"I'm not mad," insisted Betsy more quietly. She took Steve's hand and began to pull him toward her.

Jamie made a gagging sound in her throat.

"Well, that's really mature," said Betsy sharply. "You're the one who's acting weird."

" *Shut up or I'll kill you!*" screamed the man in the front row.

"Never mind," said Steve grimly. "Let's just watch the rest of the movie."

After *Fresh Graves* was over, Steve and Betsy decided to get hamburgers and french fries at a drive-in restaurant.

Jamie sat in the backseat of the car while they ate — and she was starving. As the smell of the food wafted back to her, her stomach began to rumble. Luckily Steve and Betsy were too polite to ask each other, "Was that you?" Otherwise they might have guessed that they had a stowaway in the car.

Besides being hungry, Jamie was bored. Betsy and Steve weren't mad at each other anymore, but they seemed to have decided not to try any more kissing that night. All they did was talk about a school ski trip they were planning for later in the year.

Jamie leaned forward to see the clock on the dashboard. It was ten. She'd snuck out with Betsy at seven, leaving her bedroom door closed, as if she were inside doing her homework. By now, her parents had probably noticed she was missing. . . .

Why does magic always get you into trouble? Jamie wondered. It worked out that way in stories, too. People who got three wishes usually ended up having to use the third one to get out of the trouble caused by the first two.

What was that? Jamie wondered, sitting up with a start. It looked like a bug hovering in front of her. She reached out to brush it away. But it wasn't a bug. It was her nose. Her nose — and only her nose — had turned visible again.

Horrified, Jamie edged herself forward again and peeked into the rearview mirror. Yup, that was her nose, all right!

Jamie clapped her hands over her nose. But she'd forgotten that her hands were transparent, so of course that didn't work. She ducked down behind Betsy's seat. What was she going to do?

"So if we pool all our money, we can rent a really nice ski nose," Steve droned. He paused. "I mean, ski lodge. I don't know why I said that."

He saw my nose! Jamie thought in a panic. He saw it without realizing it!

Then another thought occurred to her. What if this time she was becoming visible gradually? Maybe her nose was just a warning! Maybe the rest of her was about to follow in bits and pieces!

It would be sort of difficult to keep Betsy and Steve from noticing something like that.

"And then maybe we could hire an instructor to —" Steve paused again. "You know, I have the strangest feeling that we're not alone."

"That movie must have affected you more than you want to admit," said Betsy.

"No! I — I think I hear something breathing!"

Steve swiveled around in the driver's seat and peered into the back. Jamie lay motionless on the floor. It's dark back here, she thought, but if he turns on the light, then I'm finished. . . .

"I guess you're right, Betsy," he said after a second. "Maybe it was just my conscience," he added reluctantly. "I think it's telling me I should take you home so I can study for that math test."

Jamie went limp with relief. Hurry, she thought. In the half-light of the backseat she could see that her left thumb had turned visible again.

"I'll see you tomorrow, Steve," Betsy said a few minutes later. She opened the car door on her side.

In a flash Jamie had scrambled into the front seat, across Betsy's lap, and out the door. She had to get out of the car before Steve drove away!

"What do you think you're doing?" Betsy gasped.

Steve looked blankly at her. "Betsy, I didn't do anything!"

"Then you were right! There must have been something back there!" Betsy said. "It must have been some kind of animal!"

Jamie made her way slowly around the house, quickly forgetting Betsy and Steve as she pondered her new dilemma. There was no way she could go in the front door — not with that nose and thumb on display. She'd have to climb up the tree by her bedroom window and get in that way. And then she'd have to hope her parents bought the story that she'd been asleep in bed for hours.

I've had it with these sneakers, she thought as she started climbing. It's almost as if they're trying to embarrass me. I'm mailing them back the first chance I get.

Chapter Five

Monday mornings are never fun, but you know things are really bad when your teacher comes to school dressed as a butterfly.

"Hello, everybody," Miss Duni trilled to her astonished class as she waltzed into the room. What looked like old curtains hung from her arms to form makeshift wings. Huge antennae made of wire and feathers bobbed above her eyes.

"I thought I'd start us all off on the right foot for our first Bug Session," she said with a beaming smile. "Or maybe I should say the right six feet. As you can see, I have six legs on my thorax, like all insects." Jamie noticed that Miss Duni had sewn three pairs of stockings to her shirt. Jamie and Randy exchanged despairing glances.

"So!" Miss Duni said brightly. "Today I want us all to start thinking about insects and nothing but insects. That's why I've decided to set this whole day aside for our Bug Session. I even got permission for you to skip gym. No math! No social studies! No French! Just bugs, bugs, bugs!"

"Yay!" said Larry Berman. He always tried to be enthusiastic about Miss Duni's ideas.

The rest of the class was still staring, flabbergasted, at their teacher. But Miss Duni didn't seem to notice. "Now, as I explained last week," she continued briskly, "we'll be working in pairs for Bug Session. Each pair will study one particular insect. Then, at the end of the six weeks, each member of the team will do his or her own report. That way you get to study together, but complete your reports alone."

In other words, we get the worst of both worlds, thought Jamie. She glanced over at Bill Baird. He flared his nostrils and rolled up his eyes until only the whites showed. Shuddering, Jamie turned away.

"Okay, gang!" said Miss Duni excitedly. "I've got a big hat filled with insect names here!" Even the hat had been decorated for Bug Session — Miss Duni had sewn antennae onto it, too. "Let's have all the pairs line up so we can find out what wonderful bug will be their friend for the next six weeks!"

Larry Berman jumped to his feet and ran to the front of the room. The rest of the class followed more slowly, including Randy, who was stuck with being Larry's partner. Finally a straggling line had formed behind the hat.

Larry plunged his hand into the hat. "I wonder what insect we'll get, Randy!" he chirped. He pulled out a slip of paper and handed it to her with a flourish. "What does it say? What does it say?" he asked eagerly.

"*Earwig*," said Randy expressionlessly. Even Larry's face fell for a second.

"Earwig!" cried Miss Duni. "Oh, that's wonderful! You'll get to find out all about those dear little pinchy fellows. Then, when you see them in your house, you'll know that they're your friends! Okay, who's next?"

The next pair got bees. Too bad, Jamie thought. Bees really were interesting. In fact, she had to admit that most of the insects the kids were picking sounded interesting. Ants . . . praying mantises . . . fireflies . . . crickets . . .

Now it was Jamie and Bill's turn. "I'll pick it," Bill announced, elbowing Jamie in the ribs. He grabbed a slip of paper and turned away so that Jamie wouldn't be able to see it.

"*Drosophila*," he read slowly, looking puzzled.

Drosophila! What in the world was that? Jamie turned to Miss Duni and gave her a questioning look.

"Boy, are you two lucky," the teacher told her. "That's the Latin name for fruit flies."

Fruit flies! Jamie thought in disgust. Why couldn't we get something cute like ladybugs?

"I think you'll find that the most interesting thing about fruit flies is how often they reproduce," Miss Duni went on. "It's just *fascinating*."

52

Jamie almost collapsed with horror. She was going to have to study reproduction with Bill Baird?

"It sounds very interesting, Miss Duni," said Bill politely.

"Oh, it is," she agreed. "Now, class, I have another surprise for you." Miss Duni blushed. "Most of you may not know that I . . . well . . . I write poems. And in honor of Bug Session, I have composed several poems about insects."

"How wonderful!" said Bill Baird. He sounded even more enthusiastic than Larry Berman. "Why don't you have Jamie read them to the class, Miss Duni? She's really great at reading aloud, you know."

"Why, Bill, that's a great idea," agreed Miss Duni before Jamie could say anything. "Here, Jamie, you come and stand by my desk. The rest of you can sit down." Randy gave Jamie a heartfelt look of sympathy as Jamie slowly proceeded to the front of the room.

If only I had my sneakers now, Jamie thought. I'd rather disappear in front of everybody than read in front of them.

But the sneakers were back in their box at home, ready to be returned to Aunt Letitia as soon as Jamie could get to the post office.

Jamie took the first sheet of paper Miss Duni handed her. "The Beauty of Termites," she read aloud. Miss Duni smiled bashfully. Please,

please don't let me get a case of the giggles,
Jamie prayed. She cleared her throat and began
to read.

"Oh, when I see them gnawing,
It gnaws my heartstrings, too . . . "

"What's this?" Jamie asked, after her reading
was over. She'd managed to get through it by
concentrating on her plan to get even with Bill
the Pill.

"Looks like makeup," said Bill the Pill. "You
sure could use some, Keenan."

Actually, the little jar Miss Duni had just
handed them didn't look anything like makeup.
It was filled with tiny white specks — and they
looked as if they were moving.

"Those are fruit fly larvae," said Miss Duni. "I
asked the biology teacher in the high school if he
had any to spare. We were very lucky that he did.
I also borrowed this empty aquarium. You can
put the larvae in it with a little sugar water and
see what happens! Won't that be exciting? It's
almost like being parents, isn't it?"

"It certainly is, Miss Duni," said Bill. When
Miss Duni was safely out of earshot, he turned to
Jamie.

He stared at her face in silence for a few seconds.

"You know, I think I see a resemblance," he said.

"Look! There's a mosquito! Let's get it for the collection!" Bill Baird shouted. With a thwack he brought his butterfly net down over Jamie's head.

"Oops, sorry," he said as Jamie angrily lifted the net off. "I guess it wasn't a mosquito, after all."

Jamie rubbed her aching shoulder and trudged on, more miserable by the minute. After lunch that day, Miss Duni had given everyone in the class a net and led them outside for some outdoor research.

"A bug hunt! Good going!" Bill Baird said loudly when Miss Duni made the announcement. "We'll get to shoot a few bugs!"

"Not shoot them! Oh, no, no, no!" Miss Duni sounded very upset. "We'll just *gather* them and bring them back into the classroom alive so they can keep us company. Bugs are our buddies, you know!"

Now Miss Duni was leading them through the woods in the back of the school. And she was making them walk with their Bug Session partners.

"Look! Is that a monarch butterfly?" Jamie heard the teacher saying from the front of the line. "Oh, no, I guess it's just a leaf."

Jamie was covered with mud. Bill had tripped her while she was stepping over a puddle. Her eye was smarting from the branch he'd "accidentally" snapped in her direction when he'd barged ahead of her, and her feet were aching from the number of times he'd stepped on them.

For some reason Jamie thought of the sneakers just then. They might have come in handy on a walk like this. But of course, she was still planning on returning them. . . .

Jamie limped slowly toward her locker. School was finally over.

Jamie had never felt so tired before. The class had walked for five miles — and all they'd managed to turn up were a few ants, a wasp, and a raggedy old moth.

"We'll have better luck tomorrow," Miss Duni had said. "I'm sure some gorgeous creature will cross our path."

Jamie wasn't so sure. It seemed to her that the end of September wasn't the best time to be looking for bugs.

And if I'd worn my magic high-tops on the hike, I might not be so tired now, she thought.

"Hey, Keenan!"

Bill the Pill was standing in front of his locker, which was right next to Jamie's. "I just wanted to apologize for the way I treated you today," he said. "I — I don't know what got into me. I'm really sorry."

"Bill, I —" Jamie didn't know what to say.

"Can we shake hands?" asked Bill humbly. "Since we're going to be partners for the rest of the Bug Sessions and all?"

"Sure, I guess!" said Jamie. She could hardly believe it. Could it be that her troubles with Bill the Pill were over forever?

He walked toward her and held out his hand, so Jamie held out hers — and Bill ground a dead caterpillar into her palm.

"I found it on our nature walk," he said with a smile.

"Ugh! You stinker!" Jamie yelled.

"Why, Jamie, I'm shocked by your language," said Bill. "What a childish way to express yourself — Hey! What are you doing?"

Jamie sprang forward and wiped her caterpillar-covered hand on his shirt. Then she bolted down the hall to Randy's locker.

"W-w-wait until you hear this!" she sputtered, and poured out her story to her friend.

"Oh, that's awful!" said Randy sympathetically. "The poor caterpillar!"

"The poor caterpillar? What about poor *me*?"

"I know," said Randy. She patted Jamie on the shoulder. "It will be really hard to forgive him for this, I'll bet."

"Ran, you don't understand. I'm not going to forgive him," answered Jamie excitedly. "I've just decided to keep my new high-tops. Those sneakers and I were put together for one reason: to get revenge on Bill the Pill. From now on he's the bug — and I'm the bug zapper."

Chapter Six

Vanishing from this classroom will be a special pleasure today, thought Jamie, glancing around her. Miss Duni had been busy since yesterday — busy transforming the classroom into an insect paradise.

That is, it would have been a paradise for any insect who happened to be eight feet long. In one corner Miss Duni had attached a huge burlap chrysalis to the wall. "Later I'll choose someone to dress up and hatch out of it," she promised the class.

In another corner she'd constructed a giant anthill out of sand. Bits of it kept crumbling and rolling down onto the floor. And draped over the top of the blackboard was a huge spiderweb made of thick white twine.

"Spiders aren't insects, Miss Duni," Dan McCarthy objected when the class observed what their teacher had done.

"But I wish they were," Miss Duni answered dreamily. "It just doesn't seem possible that something as beautiful as a spiderweb wasn't made by an insect. I tell you what, kids — let's

60

call spiders insects during Bug Session so they don't feel left out. They only have two more legs than insects, after all.

"Today we're going to discuss some of the characteristics of an insect," she continued. "Now one very important trait is that they're invertebrates. That means they don't have skeletons."

"Like you, Keenan," Bill Baird whispered, grinning wickedly at Jamie.

Quickly Jamie raised her hand. "May I go to the bathroom?" she asked.

Miss Duni frowned slightly. "But we just got started, Jamie — oh, well, go ahead. Hurry back, though."

Actually, Jamie didn't plan to come back at all. At least not in her visible state. She put her pink high-tops on in the bathroom and waited until she'd disappeared. Then she headed back down the hall to the classroom.

"Is a fly an invertebrate, Miss Duni?" Randy was asking as Jamie tiptoed back into the room.

"Oh, yes. All insects are."

"What about a bee?" Randy asked.

"Yes. All insects are," Miss Duni repeated.

"Even — uh — even wasps? I think I once saw a wasp with a skeleton, didn't I?"

Jamie groaned inwardly. Try some other kind of animal! she wanted to shout at her friend. Randy was only following orders — trying to distract the class so that no one would notice in case

61

Jamie made a noise as she crept back in. But even Miss Duni was going to get impatient if Randy couldn't come up with better questions.

"Well, what about — what about ladybugs?" Randy was asking now, her voice growing fainter and fainter.

Jamie had decided that her revenge plan should start small. For now she was going to pester Bill. "Today, a mosquito," she told Randy. "Tomorrow, a shark." Holding her breath, she walked silently up to Bill's chair, unwrapped the paper towel from around the special surprise she'd sneaked off Betsy's plate at breakfast — and dropped the cold, wet grapefruit segment inside his collar.

That'll pay you back for the beetle you dropped down my back, she thought triumphantly.

"And what about —" Randy began.

"*Yiiiiiieee!*" Bill yelled, leaping straight into the air. "There's a snake in my shirt! I can feel its slimy skin!" He yanked his shirttail out and flapped it around wildly.

With a little plop the piece of grapefruit hit the floor. The room was silent as everyone stared at it.

"That's a really scary-looking snake, Bill," said Randy sweetly.

Bill stared incredulously at the blob of grapefruit. "How did *that* get in my shirt?" he asked in a dazed voice.

"You must have done it by accident while you were eating breakfast this morning," said Miss Duni.

"But we didn't *have* grapefruit for —"

"All right, class," Miss Duni interrupted. "Let's get back to invertebrates. Now, the exoskeleton is ... "

Once things settled down again Bill picked up his pencil and started doodling on a torn sheet of paper. Jamie peeked over his shoulder as he wrote THE BAIRD MINI-SUB in large capital letters. Then he began drawing plans for the submarine itself. He'd just started working on the giant spear-gun attachment when Jamie struck again.

She leaned over his shoulder and picked up his eraser. Then she hurled it at the blackboard as hard as she could.

The eraser hit the board smack in the middle of the word *exoskeleton*, bounced off, and landed on Miss Duni's foot.

"Who threw that?" she snapped. The dreamy quality in her voice was gone.

"Bill Baird did," said Leesa Alexander immediately. You could always count on Leesa to tattle. It made her a hit with young and old alike.

"I — I did?" Bill asked. "I mean, I did not!"

"I saw it. You did it," said Leesa. "You could have hurt Miss Duni, you know. I don't think

63

jokes that hurt people are very funny, do you? What if —"

"All right, Leesa," said Miss Duni tiredly. She glanced at her watch and sighed. "Bill, pipe down."

Even Jamie thought that was a little unfair. Bill hadn't piped *up*. His mouth was moving, but no sound was coming out. He looked like a fish who'd just been hit by a truck.

But Jamie didn't feel that sorry for Bill — not nearly sorry enough to stop this early in the game.

"Okay, gang! Move it on out! Ten times around the track!" bellowed Mr. Norquist, Jamie's gym teacher. He clapped his hands ferociously. With each clap, drops of sweat flew off his face.

I don't know how he gets so sweaty when we're the ones who have to do all the exercise, thought Jamie. But she wasn't going to complain. This was the first time she'd looked forward to gym class all year.

It was two hours after the grapefruit incident, and a blazing Indian-summer sun was beating down on the track at Laughing Egg Elementary. Gym had just started — or, rather, *not* started. Everyone in Miss Duni's class was sprawled in the hot grass except for Mr. Norquist, the gym teacher.

"Get going!" Mr. Norquist shouted again.

Everyone groaned, but nobody moved. "It's too roasting to run around the bases," Marlene Heiklen muttered.

"It's too roasting to *walk* around them," said Peter Burbank. Peter hated exercise. He'd managed to convince his mother that he was too weak to walk to the bus stop two houses away from his own, so she drove him to school every day.

"Come on!" Mr. Norquist hollered again. "Up and at 'em!"

Slowly everyone stood up.

"That means you, too, bug-head," Bill Baird said to Jamie. "If you can run three steps without falling on your face, that is. Even though it would probably improve your face to have dirt on it."

Jamie just smiled at him.

"What are *you* so happy about?" he growled.

"Oh, the future," she answered as she started off around the track.

Jamie was probably the only person in the class who was glad they had to run for so long a distance. She'd put her sneakers back on twenty minutes before gym had begun, so she was due to disappear any minute now — and hopefully everyone around her would be huffing and puffing too hard to notice.

That's just the way it happened. By the time the class had collapsed back onto the grass again, no one except Randy realized that Jamie was missing. And when softball practice started, no one knew that the Invisible Avenger was shadowing Bill Baird as he stepped up to the plate.

Mike Liu was pitching. He threw the first ball — an easy pitch that went straight toward Billy's bat.

"Go for it, Baird!" shouted Mr. Norquist.

Just as Bill swung, Jamie jumped up and grabbed the tip of the bat. She pulled it down as hard as she could — and held it there.

The class didn't know she was holding it, of course. All they saw was Bill wrestling with a baseball bat. And from what they could see, the bat was winning the match.

"This bat's too heavy!" Bill hollered at last, dropping it.

"Baird, you can't be serious! It's the lightest one we have!" said Mr. Norquist. He shook his head. "Some athlete. Strike one!"

The next time Bill swung, Jamie gave him a little shove between the shoulder blades — just enough to put him off balance so that he toppled forward into the dust.

But she didn't make him strike out. She let him hit the third pitch. Then she raced to first base and stationed herself right in front of the bag.

Bill ran right into her. "*Ooooof!*" he grunted.

66

No one noticed the ball hit the grass. They were all staring at Bill — wondering why he'd come to a full stop two feet in front of the base.

Bill looked at the empty space in front of the plate totally confused. He tried to move forward, but Jamie held her ground.

"Baird, what is going on?" shouted Mr. Norquist.

Bill looked helplessly up at him. "I don't know," he said. "The — the air just got solid all of a sudden."

Mr. Norquist strode angrily up to first base. Jamie jumped out of the way as he swished his hands through the air where she'd just been standing.

"Solid, huh?" he said disgustedly. "I'll tell you what's solid, pal. The space between your ears! You're out!"

Jamie took the sneakers off after gym and put them on just before lunch. Luck was with her this time — she disappeared immediately.

Jamie couldn't stand the food at school, so she always brought her lunch from home. Bill, on the other hand, always bought the school lunches. Just another sign of how disgusting he really is, Jamie thought.

She stood in back of him in the lunch line and watched as he loaded up his plate with mushy grayish-white stuff that was supposedly spaghetti. Then he took three bags of potato chips and three chocolate milk cartons. He cracked open one of the milks and began drinking it right out of the carton.

Jamie gave him a little push. Not a hard one — just hard enough to make him splash chocolate milk all over his face.

"Hey, quit pushing!" Bill said, turning around to see who was in back of him.

He didn't see Jamie, of course. He saw the person in back of her — Mike Demado, the biggest and toughest kid in fourth grade.

"Oh, hi, Mike!" Bill said with a nervous giggle. "I didn't mean you! Come to think of it, no one pushed me. I guess I'm just — just a butterfingers today! Hee-hee-hee!"

He was still holding the carton of chocolate milk. As Mike watched, Jamie grabbed Bill's hand and made him empty the carton all over Mike's tray.

The color drained out of Bill's face. "I — I'm sorry," he said, backing slowly out of the line. His teeth were actually chattering. "Just a — butterfingers, as I said. Whoops! I think I hear the bell. Lunch is over! Too bad!" He grabbed his tray and rushed toward the cafeteria door.

It was easy for Jamie to trip him — but she hadn't expected such a spectacular fall. Bill flipped over backward. His tray flew into the air. The plate of spaghetti landed on his head, and he landed on one of the chocolate milk cartons. It burst with a loud pop all over the seat of his jeans.

Behind Jamie, Mike Demado shook his head in amazement. "I won't beat him up, after all," he muttered. "The guy's done enough damage to himself. He needs help."

Slowly, Bill struggled to his feet with the whole cafeteria watching him.

I guess I'll go take off my sneakers, Jamie thought. I should get some lunch myself.

Suddenly she was starving. The sneakers were going to be fun, after all. For the first time since the school year had begun, Jamie felt herself begin to relax.

Even the most obnoxious boy in the world was no match for an invisible girl.

Chapter Seven

For the next few days Bill Baird left Jamie alone. He seemed to be too confused and upset by what had happened to him to pay attention to her or anyone else. Mostly he just walked around shaking his head. It was a very satisfying sight.

School went fine once the class had managed to convince Miss Duni that *they* shouldn't have to come to school in bug costumes. The only thing Jamie used the sneakers for was to play invisible sports after school. It was the first chance she'd ever had to play the games she loved without embarrassing herself.

All in all, Jamie was in a great mood. But for some reason Randy began to look more and more bothered as the days went on. "What's the matter?" Jamie finally asked her.

"Have you gotten anything unusual in the mail?" was Randy's surprising answer.

"No," said Jamie. "Not unless you call letters from my grandmother unusual. Why? Have you?"

Randy sighed sadly. "No," she said. "That's the problem. Starr Stuart is having a slumber party next week, and it looks as though neither of us has been invited."

Every girl in school wanted to be Starr Stuart's friend. Starr had long blond hair, more clothes than Jamie and Randy combined, and her own VCR. She had appeared in a commercial for the Doughnuteria on Main Street, and she was a champion horseback rider. She'd even gotten to study butterflies for Bug Session.

And she never let anyone forget any of these things, which was why Jamie and Randy couldn't stand her.

"So we miss one party!" said Jamie with a shrug. "It's not the worst thing in the world!"

But over the next few days it started to seem that way. Starr wasn't the kind of girl to keep a party quiet.

"We're going to send out for pizza," Jamie heard her telling Judy Gollin on the school bus. "And I've reserved seven videos, and my parents say we can stay up as late as we want. They promised to stay upstairs the whole time. And I thought maybe we could have a séance. . . . "

Then Starr noticed Jamie watching her. "Ssshhh! A fruit fly is listening!" she hissed sharply, pointing at Jamie. She and Judy both giggled. Then they put their heads together and started whispering.

Okay, Starr, Jamie said to herself. You've gone too far this time.

"I think Starr's going to be very surprised on Saturday night," Jamie said to Randy after school that day as they walked home.

"Why?"

"Well, there's going to be an unexpected guest at her party," Jamie said innocently. "Two of them, actually. One will be the Invisible Avenger. Can you guess who the other one is going to be?"

"Jamie, what are you talking about? I'm not crashing Starr's party! I have some pride, you know!"

"Now, Randy. We're not going to crash it. We're just going to help Starr throw a party she'll never forget."

"But that's mean!" Randy protested. "She doesn't have to invite us to her party if she doesn't want to! My mother says we should be mature about this!"

At that very moment Starr rode up behind them on her bicycle. "I've been looking all over for you guys!" she panted. "Are you doing anything on Saturday night?"

Randy's eyes brightened. Was Starr going to invite them, after all? "We're not doing anything at all!" she said happily.

"Well, I just wanted to tell you there's a really good documentary about termites on public television that night," said Starr. "You guys should try and catch it. It's better than doing nothing!"

Starr's shoulders were shaking with laughter as she pedaled away.

Jamie and Randy stood watching Starr ride away in silence. "As I was saying, Jamie, my mother thinks we should be mature about this," Randy said finally. "And I agree with her. I think the most mature thing we could do would be to put aside our pride and go to the party, after all. What exactly did you have in mind?"

Lightning crackled overhead as Randy and Jamie arrived at Starr's house. The wind moaned and whipped the girls' dripping hair into their eyes. The streets were slick and black with rain, and from far off in the distance came the ominous boom of thunder.

Their parents wouldn't have liked them to be out in this weather — but what their parents didn't know wouldn't hurt them. Jamie had told the Keenans she'd be spending the evening at Randy's. Randy had told her family she'd be spending the evening at Jamie's. Now both of them were on their way to Starr's. Luckily Starr lived just down the block from the Dowells.

Jamie was already invisible. She'd put her magic sneakers on fifteen minutes before. "Now, do you remember what you're supposed to say?" she asked Randy.

"Y-y-y-yes," said Randy. Her teeth were chattering. "I know it so well I almost believe it myself! Here's Starr's house."

"Okay," said Jamie. "You knock and go right into your act. When you're all done, go around the side of the house and wait by the livingroom window. I'll meet you as soon as I can. Good luck!"

"Th-th-thanks." Randy shivered as she reached forward and banged the brass lion's-head knocker. Once. Twice. Three times — and Starr opened the door halfway.

"Randy Dowell!" she said. "What are you doing here?"

Randy's face was white with terror. "I know you're having a party," she gasped. "But could I come in for just a second? I think that escaped murderer was chasing me!"

"What escaped murderer?" Starr demanded.

"Didn't you hear about it on the news?" said Randy. "There's a murderer from the prison who dug his way out of his cell with a kitchen knife! And the police say he's in our neighborhood!"

Starr turned pale, too. She pulled Randy inside and slammed the door so fast that Jamie barely made it in after her.

Starr's guests were lounging around the living room watching a video. There were pizza boxes and cans of soda everywhere. But the girls

74

gathered around in shocked silence as a trembling Randy continued her story.

"I was walking home when this shadowy-looking guy started following me," she said. "I thought I'd lost him, but when I passed your house I saw him again. He was hiding in the bushes — and I think he was holding a knife!"

A horribly loud crack of thunder seemed to explode just overhead. Everyone jumped, and Megan Stern gave a little shriek.

"It's just a little thunder, girls," Starr's father called jovially from upstairs. "Don't let things get out of hand down there."

"Yes," Randy said dully. "Just a little thunder." She shuddered, then seemed to pull herself together. "Well, I've got to go home now," she said. "Thanks for letting me in, Starr."

"Wait! You can't go out there!" said Starr. "Don't you want some pizza or something? It's kind of congealed, but —"

"No, thanks," Randy said bravely. "I have to get home. The longer I wait in here, the more scared I'll get."

She walked to the door and stared at the girls in the room as though she were seeing them for the last time.

"Wish me luck," she said in a husky voice, and vanished into the night.

Chapter Eight

Starr dashed forward and locked the door. Then she turned back to her friends.

"I — I'm sure there's no one out there anymore," she said. "It's much too rainy for anyone to stay outside for very long."

She's scared, Jamie decided, but she doesn't want this party ruined. She's going to try to keep things going. I may have to work harder than I thought.

Starr clapped her hands as though she were trying to cheer herself up. "Well, the fun must go on! Who wants to have a séance?" she asked.

Silence.

"A séance *now*?" asked Judy Gollin.

"Well, sure!" said Starr. "I thought we all wanted one!"

"That was before we heard the . . . news," said Megan Stern faintly. "Maybe we should call Randy's house and make sure she got home."

"Oh, come on!" said Starr. "We're not going to let a little story about an escaped murderer — I mean — we're not going to let a rainy night spoil

76

my party, are we? Come on," she said briskly. "Everyone sit in a circle."

Starr was used to getting her way. Slowly her friends obeyed. "Okay," said Starr, "time to put out the lights." She leaned over and flicked the overhead light switch. The room plunged into darkness except for the flickers of lightning outside.

"Do we *have* to keep the lights out?" Megan asked.

"Yes! It's my party!" snapped Starr. "Now, whose spirit shall we raise from the dead?"

On the other hand, Jamie thought gleefully, maybe I won't have to work so hard after all. Starr's doing a great job of scaring people herself!

No one seemed to have any suggestions for whom to raise from the dead.

"All right," said Starr. "I guess I don't have any choice. I'll have to think of the spirit. And I say it should be . . . " She paused for a moment. "I say it should be Elvis Presley."

"*Elvis Presley!*" Jamie exclaimed before she could stop herself.

"What's wrong with him?" Starr said defensively. "He was a really important guy, and he had a big stable and his own plane and . . . Wait a minute. Who said that, anyway?"

No one answered.

"Well, *okay*. If you're afraid to confess, then who cares what you think," said Starr. "Anyway, let's call up his spirit."

"How?" asked Gretchen Braverman.

"First we join hands." Reluctantly the girls did as Starr asked.

"Now we say his name over and over," Starr went on.

"*Elvis Presley*," Lucy Mulhrony blared out.

A wave of giggles swept the circle. "Not like that, Lucy!" Starr said angrily. "You have to say it more in a — in a *trance* kind of way. Like this: Ellllviiiiiis . . . Elllviiiiiis . . . "

"Elllviiiiiis," the girls began to chant. "Elllviiiiiis. Elllviiiiiis. Elllviiiiiis."

"Then what happens?" someone whispered.

"We keep saying it. And we keep thinking it," said Starr in a singsong voice. "We remember everything we can about him. And then his spirit will come."

Jamie stepped into the center of the circle and sat down.

The girls' chanting stopped instantly. "Wh-what was that?" Megan Stern quavered.

"I felt some kind of weird breeze," whispered Judy Gollin.

"I felt it, too!" Starr sounded excited — and a little surprised. "We must really have done it! We raised a spirit from the dead! *Elvis is here!*"

"You girls want some cookies or something?" called Starr's mother from upstairs.

"No, Mom!" Starr shouted impatiently. "We're busy!"

"Okay, honey, but help yourselves if you get hungry!"

"She always butts in," Starr muttered. Then she cleared her throat and slipped back into her mystical voice.

"Elvis . . . are you on the other side? That means the other side of the grave," she added in her normal voice. "We would like to communicate with you. Knock once for yes, twice for no. Are you with the spirits now?"

Jamie rapped the floor once.

"Are you happy on the other side?"

No, Jamie knocked.

"No? Why not? Oh, I guess I have to ask a yes-or-no question. Do you miss your family?"

No.

"Do you miss your horses?"

No.

"Is it — is it fun on the other side?" Judy whispered.

No.

Jamie's knuckles were starting to hurt.

"Will you sing us one of your hits?" put in Lucy.

No.

Starr gave Judy a surreptitious kick. "Elvis, do you have any messages for us?"

Yes.

"Good ones?"

No.

This could take forever! Jamie decided to speed things up a little. "Waaaaaaaarrniiiiii-ing . . . " she wailed in a whisper.

"He *spoke!*" whispered Starr.

The rest of the girls shifted uneasily. "Warning? What kind of warning?" asked Gretchen. "A warning for us?"

"Daaaaaaanger . . . " wailed Jamie. "Prisoner . . . "

Every girl in the circle gasped.

"What prisoner?" Starr asked sharply.

"*Murderer!*"

Every girl in the circle screamed.

"Keep it *down,* girls!" shouted Mr. Stuart angrily.

"Stop this, Starr. Please stop this," moaned Megan, hiding her head in her lap.

"N-no. W-we have to find out what he means!" Starr was almost sobbing. "Elvis, is the murderer h-h-here?"

"Wiiiindooooow," Jamie sighed.

"Oh, no!" Now Starr was really crying. So was everyone else in the room. "I — I'm going up to get my daddy," Starr wept.

Uh-oh, Jamie thought. If Mr. Stuart comes down he'll wreck everything! She jumped noiselessly to her feet and ran across the room to the window.

"Look at the windoooow," she whispered. The terrified girls turned to the window — and saw Randy's dark head silhouetted there. Then Jamie wrenched the window open.

Never in the history of Laughing Egg had there been a scream as loud as the one that came from Starr and her friends at that moment.

"All right! I've had it with you young ladies!"

It was Starr's father. He came stomping down the stairs and stormed into the living room.

"What's going on here?" he bellowed. "Why are the lights out? Why is the window open? What's all this caterwauling about?"

Starr rushed up and flung her arms around her father's waist.

"Elvis . . . the window . . . the murderer . . . a kitchen knife!" she howled. "He's out there! He's going to get us!"

"I don't know what you're talking about," said Mr. Stuart coldly. "I only know one thing. This party is over. I'm taking you girls home right now."

If Starr's friend had looked out of the car window on their way home, they might have seen Jamie and Randy skipping triumphantly down the street to Randy's house.

81

"Oh, Ran, you should have seen yourself!" said Jamie. "You looked so creepy! I almost screamed too!"

"Well, you should have seen Starr's face when you opened the window," Randy said, giggling. "I wish I could have climbed in instead of having to duck out of the way."

"We can save that for another party," said Jamie. She sighed happily. "But somehow I don't think Starr's going to have another one for a very long time."

Chapter Nine

A few days later, Miss Duni's class came into the room one morning to find a very dejected teacher. She was standing in the front of the room with her head hanging down. Even the antennae she'd sewn to her hairband looked droopy.

"I'm afraid we won't be able to concentrate on Bug Session today, people," she said dolefully. "We've got to go on a field trip. As some of you may know, Bill Baird's father owns a candy factory just outside of Laughing Egg." Bill looked around the room smugly.

"Mr. Baird has been kind enough to invite our class to visit the factory," said Miss Duni. "And I guess today's the day. I'd much rather have you stay in school and work on your insect studies, but the principal seems to think this trip will be educational for us."

Miss Duni looked amazed when the whole class erupted into cheers. Even Jamie was delighted. Of course she had to hate a factory owned by any relative of Bill the Pill — but the trip had to be more fun than a Bug Session.

"The buses are outside," Miss Duni told the class gloomily. "Let's go put on our cocoons — I mean our coats. And no running in the halls."

Shouting and laughing, the kids in the class jumped up, pushed their way through the door, and raced down the hall to their lockers. Miss Duni followed slowly, shaking her head.

"Isn't this great?" Jamie exclaimed when she caught up with Randy. "A whole day without fruit flies!"

"It's fantastic," said Randy. Suddenly she caught sight of what Jamie was carrying. "You're not going to bring along those sneakers, I hope," she said.

"Of course I am!" said Jamie. "How can I pass up the chance to be invisible at a candy factory?"

"But, Jamie," said Randy in a worried voice. "I know you. . . . You'll probably touch all the candy. What about germs?"

"Oh, I'm not worried about them," said Jamie. "Those kinds of places are always very clean."

"No, that's not what I meant! The problem is your germs getting into candy that the factory has to sell!"

"Oh," said Jamie, crestfallen. "Well, I'll be really careful. Ran. I promise. I'll only touch what I plan to eat."

"Just save me some," Randy said.

"Don't fall into any of the vats at my father's factory," Bill told Jamie as they got off the bus. "We don't want to poison the whole country."

"*Hello, everybody!*" boomed a huge voice from the front entrance of the factory. "*Welcome to Baird's beautiful world of candy!*"

Startled, Jamie turned around. A massive man in a white uniform was standing in the doorway. He looked exactly like Bill except for the fact that he was about four hundred pounds heavier.

"I bet that's Miss Duni!" he shouted, grabbing the teacher's hand. "Glad to meetcha! My boy's told me all about you!"

"I — I'm Miss Duni," said Miss Duni. She shook hands with Mr. Baird. "My," she said politely, "you certainly are a good advertisement for your products!"

"Oh, you mean candy? Love the stuff. Eat it all the time — a couple of pounds a day," said Mr. Baird. "It's good for you, you know. You look a little skinny. Well, c'mon in, everybody! Come meet your tour guide!"

The tour guide was a stooped, pinched-looking man named Mr. Tweedie who kept blinking behind thick glasses.

"Tweedie'll tell you everything you need to know!" said Mr. Baird enthusiastically, slapping Mr. Tweedie's shoulders so hard he almost knocked him down. "Well, back to work." As Mr.

85

Baird stomped away, the whole building seemed to shudder.

"He's very busy," said Bill Baird proudly. "Much busier than the rest of your fathers, I'll bet."

"Now, children, please gather 'round," said Mr. Tweedie in a high-pitched whining voice. "I'm sure you are all aware of the many roles candy plays in our society, from Halloween treats to that lovely gift box for Grandma. Candy is . . . "

"Are we going to get any free samples?" someone called out.

Mr. Tweedie frowned slightly. "I believe there is a complimentary gumball at the end of the tour," he said. "Now, candy, or confectionery, as I prefer to call it, is . . ."

I think now's the time to put on my high-tops, Jamie said to herself. She drifted to the edge of the group, rubbed her heel as if she had a blister, and sat down on a bench to change her shoes. This time she disappeared right away — but no one noticed. Everyone was dutifully listening to Mr. Tweedie. Jamie tucked her loafers under the bench so she could pick them up later.

"Now, the first place we'll be visiting is the label room," said Mr. Tweedie. "Here the very important work of printing labels is done. . . . "

To Jamie, the smell of chocolate wafting down the hall was a lot more tempting than a bunch of labels. She was sorry to leave Randy in the clutches of Mr. Tweedie, but she couldn't resist following the smell of chocolate.

At the end of the hall was a set of double doors. On one of them was a sign that read, Chocolate Enrobing in Progress. Visitors Keep Out!

Oh, well, the sign doesn't say anything about me, Jamie reassured herself. She pushed the door open a crack, and almost fell down when she saw the wonderful sight inside.

In the center of the huge room was a vat of melted chocolate the size of a school bus. The chocolate was being pumped to machines all over the room.

Right in front of Jamie was a conveyor belt covered with hundreds of undipped candy bars. As they moved slowly along, melted chocolate from long pipes poured over the various fillings. In another part of the huge room, a machine that looked like a huge pair of tweezers was dunking cherries into a smaller vat of chocolate and set-ting them onto another conveyor belt.

Empty molds in all kinds of shapes — Santa Clauses, rabbits, baby booties — were being filled with chocolate in a third section. Fresh batches of chocolate chips were being funneled into crisp new bags. There was even a rack of chocolate-covered pretzels.

If there hadn't been any people working in the room, Jamie would have had a great time. Unfortunately, there were workers all over the place.

I'll just have to be quick, Jamie decided. She slid up to the conveyor belt of chocolate-covered cherries and popped a couple into her mouth.

"Hey!" said a man a few feet away from her who was inspecting the finished cherries. "Something's wrong with this belt! It's destroying the merchandise!"

But by the time another inspector had come over, Jamie had moved on to the candy bars she'd sighted earlier. Regretfully, she decided she'd better not tackle the ones that had just been dipped. They'd be too messy. She'd have to concentrate on the insides instead. She grabbed a coconut center, a nougat-and-caramel center, and a horrible center made of rum.

Then she ran over to the chocolate chips and stuck her hand under the funnel. Chocolate chips rained into her hands. But before she could close her fists, they'd also rained all over the floor. Another inspector looked up, startled.

It's time to move on, Jamie decided, stuffing the chocolate chips into her pocket. No need to press my luck when there are so many different candies to try.

In the next room, two huge mechanical arms were tossing an enormous mass of sticky pinkish goo back and forth. As Jamie watched, the goo turned paler and smoother, until it became a satiny mass of taffy. The two arms divided it into balls, stretched each ball into a long ribbon, and cut the ribbons into tiny pillows. Jamie put a handful of them into her pocket and another handful into her mouth.

Still chewing, Jamie headed down another hall to a room where thousands of jelly beans were being painted with a glaze to make them hard and shiny. Her jaw was starting to hurt and her teeth felt as if they were stuck together, to say nothing of the stomachache she felt starting. Still, it would have seemed wasteful to leave jelly beans — her favorite candy — behind. Jamie managed to cram about thirty of them into her pocket, along with the taffy and the chocolate chips.

I should get back, Jamie decided. I'll just see what's behind this one door. . . .

Crash!

"Oh, no!" yelled someone inside the room. "That vat of lollipop syrup tipped over! We've got to get someone to help us clean it up before it hardens!"

Jamie jumped out of the way just in time as two women came racing out the door. Cautiously, she peeked around it to see what was inside. Then she tiptoed into the room.

Inside the room were pots of bubbling syrup in several different colors. For some reason, one of the pots — the one with the grape-flavored syrup

89

— had been taken off its burner and placed by the door. That was what Jamie had knocked over. And that was what she was standing in the middle of now.

Jamie lifted her right foot out of the sticky pool of syrup. Then she put it back down again to try to lift her left foot. Her left foot wouldn't budge. And when she tried again, neither would her right. She was stuck fast in a puddle of lollipop syrup.

As Jamie stood there trying to decide what to do, she suddenly heard a voice down the hall. "And in this room we prepare the chocolate confectionery. You will observe that . . . "

It was Mr. Tweedie! And he was leading the class toward the lollipop room!

Now was not the best time for Jamie to turn visible again. Needless to say, she did.

"*Jamie!*" came a voice behind her. "I knew you'd get into trouble!"

"Oh, Randy!" Jamie wanted to cry with relief. "I'm so glad it's you! I thought it was going to be one of the people who was working in here!"

"I saw them running to get a mop," said Randy. "One of them said that there was no explanation for something spilling. I didn't know what they were talking about, but I figured you were probably the one who'd done it. Is this what they were talking about?" She gestured down at the purple syrup.

"Yes. And I'm stuck in it," said Jamie.

"But Jamie, Mr. Tweedie will be here any minute now!" Randy said frantically. "We've got to get you out of here!" She reached forward and began tugging at Jamie's left arm, but before Jamie could stop her, Randy had stepped into the puddle herself.

"*No*! Randy, you'll —"

Too late. Randy was stuck, too.

"And in here we'll find a most interesting process for pulling taffy," came Mr. Tweedie's voice. "No, I've answered that question before, as you very well know. There are no free samples besides the complimentary gumball *at the end of the tour*. Step this way, please."

Jamie and Randy stared at each other in horror. "What are we going to do?" breathed Randy.

"We're going to bluff our way out of this," answered Jamie. "Help!" she shrieked. "Help us, somebody!"

"*Jamie*!" Randy hissed. "What are you doing?"

"What else can we do?" Jamie hissed back. "I'll think of something to say!"

The sound of the footsteps came thundering toward them. In a second the door opened and Mr. Tweedie came in. Behind him stood the rest of Miss Duni's class, wide-eyed.

"What is the meaning of —" Mr. Tweedie began.

Jamie cut him off. "Help us! Help us!" she wailed. She nudged Randy fiercely. After a second Randy began wailing, too.

"We got — we got lost!" Jamie said, trying as hard as she could to sound pathetic. "We came into this room by mistake and stepped in some kind of — some kind of horrible sticky stuff! There was no one in the room to help us!"

"How could you get lost?" Billy's father boomed at them. "Why didn't you follow Mr. Tweedie the way he told you to?"

"We *did,*" said Jamie indignantly. "That is, we tried to. But he was so boring that — that I guess we both dozed off and wandered in the wrong direction."

"Sleepwalking, I suppose?" said Mr. Tweedie sourly.

Jamie didn't pay any attention to him. "Also, we were getting kind of faint from hunger," she said. "It's horrible to have to walk and walk and walk for so long, without a single bite to eat . . . "

Now there were murmurs of agreement from her classmates.

"My parents aren't going to like it when they hear that we had to do all that walking without a single free sample," said Jamie in a wavering voice. "It made me awfully weak. In fact, I think I'm about to pass out right now." And she collapsed gracefully into the thick purple syrup.

"I've got to hand it to you, Jamie," said Randy happily. "You're very quick on your feet. Even when you can't *move* them."

They were on the bus headed back to school along with the rest of Miss Duni's class. Mr. Baird had agreed to let them shower in the factory locker room. And he'd given each member of the class a shopping bag full of free samples. Jamie thought he was trying to make sure no one told their parents he'd tried to starve them.

"Look at all this stuff!" Randy marveled. "Chocolate chips . . . taffy . . . jelly beans . . . "

Suddenly Jamie remembered something. "My pockets!" she gasped. "I forgot all about the stuff in my pockets!" She reached down to check them.

Her hand came up covered with a sticky, melted mass of chocolate chips, taffy, jelly beans, and shredded bits of Kleenex.

"You know, Ran, you can have my bag of samples," Jamie said. "All of a sudden I'm not hungry anymore."

Chapter Ten

"Well, class, I must say our new principal, Mr. Herman, is not very sympathetic to the idea of Bug Sessions."

Miss Duni sniffed angrily. "But since Mr. Herman has asked all of us to be present at the assembly, I suppose I must do as he says. So let's line up at the door and walk slowly to the auditorium."

Everyone leaped up and raced out the door. Today's school assembly was a big relief. As Jamie and Randy took their seats in the auditorium, Jamie felt a shiver of excitement. "I wonder what Mr. Herman wants to talk to us about," she said.

"Behavior problems on the playground, maybe?" Randy suggested.

"No, it's too early in the year for that. They always have discipline assemblies around February. Maybe he's planning a class trip to New York City or something! That would be great!"

But Mr. Herman wasn't planning a trip. He was planning a schoolwide field day to take place in two weeks.

"As you guys all know, I think student fitness is the name of the game — no pun intended," he announced. "That's why we now have gym every single day."

There were groans from the audience. A paper airplane zoomed past Mr. Herman's ear and fell to the stage, but he ignored it. "And I want Laughing Egg to be the fittest school in the district. So we'll be having these field days every season. And I want us all to be ready for them! Okay, team? Let's hear it for Laughing Egg fitness! *All right!*"

"Okay, class! Up and at 'em!" barked Mr. Norquist. "Let' moving! Ten times around the track!"

The kids in Jamie's class struggled to their feet and began loping halfheartedly around the track. Watching them, Mr. Norquist turned red with rage.

"Put a little spring in your step!" he yelled. "You're a disgrace! You want to embarrass me on Field Day, or what?"

"Yes. We do," puffed Randy crossly as she ran along. "This whole Field Day thing is exhausting me before it even starts. I swear, Jamie — I think I understand why you don't like sports."

It wasn't like Randy to talk that way. She was a great athlete, she loved gym, and she had a lot of school spirit. Besides, she almost never complained.

"Oh, it's not that bad," puffed Jamie. "I'm kind of looking forward to Field Day, actually."

Randy slowed to a trot and stared at Jamie. "Have we switched bodies or what?" she asked. "*You're* saying the kind of thing *I* usually say! How can you be looking forward to Field Day?"

"I'll be wearing my magic high-tops, of course!"

"I know they make you more athletic — but if you're invisible at Field Day, no one will be able to tell that you won a race!"

"Yes, but there's usually a gap between the time I put them on and the time I turn invisible," Jamie said. "I'll just make sure to be in all the early races. And maybe I'll win a couple for once!"

Just then Starr Stuart raced by them, her ponytail bouncing. As usual, she didn't even look sweaty. "Elvis . . ." Jamie wailed as she ran past. Starr jerked to a standstill and turned to stare at her in shock.

"Stuart! Get the lead out of your shoes!" bellowed Mr. Norquist. "Look, you just let Keenan and Dowell beat you!"

And that's only the beginning, Jamie thought happily.

"Six, seven, eight, nine, *ten*. Jamie, you did it! You got over all the hurdles!"

Jamie pushed the hair out of her eyes and smiled. "Ran, you're the best, best friend ever," she said. "I can't believe you're doing all this for me. How am I ever going to make it up to you?"

There was one week left until Field Day, and Randy had decided to spend it being Jamie's coach. Every day after school they met in Randy's yard to practice. And thanks to the sneakers, Jamie was performing incredibly well.

"Oh, you don't have to make it up to me," said Randy. "I'm sure you'll do me a favor sometime."

"Of course!" said Jamie. "How about right now? Do you want to try my sneakers?" She plunked herself down on the ground and started to unlace the left one.

"No! Not now!" said Randy hastily. "Maybe some other time. I mean, what if they make you invisible, but they turn me into a gorilla? I'm not sure I'd be ready for that! I'll tell you when I want to borrow them, I promise."

The two girls had made sure to time the intervals from the moment Jamie put the sneakers on until she finally disappeared. Usually she stayed visible for at least ten minutes before she began to fade. That meant if she waited until the exact moment Field Day started to put the sneakers on, she'd have a chance to shine in at least a couple of the events before she vanished.

"There's one thing I'm worried about, though," said Randy. "What if you suddenly disappear in the middle of a race?"

"Oh, I've thought about that," Jamie answered. "Can you trip and pretend to be hurt? That should distract everyone's attention from me."

"It certainly would," Randy said tartly. "No, Jamie. I can't go that far — even for you. You'll just have to hope it doesn't happen."

Uh-oh, Jamie thought remorsefully, I've gone too far. Randy was already being nice enough to coach her. Quickly Jamie changed the subject. "Have you finished your bug project? I can't believe Miss Duni said we had to have them ready the day after Field Day." To everyone's horror, Miss Duni had decided to move up the deadline on the projects without explaining why. "As if we didn't have enough to think about already!"

"I know," said Randy, sighing. "I hate to say it, but I bet she's trying to . . . well . . . to steal us away from Field Day. Maybe she thinks that if we have to turn in our projects early, we'll concentrate our energy on them instead of on the sports events. Anyway, I've finished my collage, so I guess I'm ready."

Randy had made a collage showing all places earwigs could be found in the home. She always did collages for class projects.

"What about you, Jamie?" she asked.

Jamie sighed. She hated deadlines. No matter how much she vowed to get things prepared ahead of time, she always found herself panicking at the last minute. "I still haven't thought of anything," she said. "I'm waiting for an idea to leap into my brain. This is definitely a bad time for Miss Duni to protest the new fitness program! I can tell Bill hasn't thought of anything, either," she went on.

"How can you tell?" asked Randy.

Jamie grinned. "Because he says he's all done."

"How are all your little fruit flies doing?" cooed in class the next day.

"Fine, thank you, Miss Duni," Bill the Pill answered politely. "I'm certainly enjoying this project, even if Jamie isn't. Would you like to look inside the aquarium you gave us?"

"I certainly would. Why, look at all of them!"

The fruit flies were doing *too* well. They loved the sugar water Jamie and Bill fed them every day, and the aquarium was filled with a dancing cloud of them. Every time Bill jiggled the lid — which he did a lot, to drive Jamie crazy — a few fruit flies managed to get out through the crack.

And they always seemed to hover maddeningly above Jamie's desk. That was because Bill had hidden an apple core in it. By the time Jamie found the apple core and threw it out, the flies had decided to settle in for good.

Miss Duni didn't mind, of course — and the other kids in the class didn't even notice. They were having too many insect problems of their own. Randy's earwigs kept crawling into her shoes. The bees kept stinging people, and the school's custodian was making a terrible fuss about the termites. "If I find any wood shavings in my walls, I'm going to hit this place with a whole case of insecticide!" he had told Miss Duni two days ago.

"You do that and I'll report you to the ASPCA," she replied icily. "My goodness, I never heard of so many people trying to get in the way of a little knowledge."

"Miss Duni, Jamie's had a very excellent idea," Bill was saying now. "She'd like to take the fruit flies home once Bug Sessions are over so she can study them some more and maybe learn to like them a little better."

"How nice! What a thoughtful gesture, Jamie," said Miss Duni before Jamie could tell her Bill was making the whole thing up. "I'll drop the aquarium off at your house myself."

Bill, I only hope you're prepared to do your best on Field Day, Jamie thought. Because I'm certainly prepared to do my best to make sure you lose every race you're in.

Chapter Eleven

"Okay, people," bellowed Mr. Norquist. "Let's get started!"

Field Day was here at last. Laughing Egg's playing fields were covered with kids in gym uniforms. The sun was beaming on the playing field as if it approved of what was going on down there. And Jamie couldn't wait for the races to start.

It's so great to know you're going to win! she thought. If this is the way real athletes feel, no wonder there are Olympic Games.

All around her, people were struggling to put T-shirts on over their uniforms. Doughnuteria on Main Street had donated shirts for everyone. There was only one problem: no one in the fourth grade especially felt like wearing them because they were skintight and hot pink. Starr Stuart, of course, looked great in hers, but she was the only one.

"The first race will start in five minutes! Get ready for the Egg Race!" called Mr. Norquist.

"I think I'm going to be sick," said Krystal Kincaid.

"Maybe you should run in the Sack Race, Krystal," Jamie suggested. "That way you won't have to stop if you do get sick."

Jamie herself was planning to be in the Egg Race, which was the very first race of the program. She got up from the grass and waved at Randy. (That was Jamie's special signal to let Randy know she was about to put on her magic sneakers.) Then Jamie casually sauntered over to the side of the field where she'd left her high-tops.

"Break a leg," said Bill the Pill as she passed him. "And an egg."

"Sure will," Jamie answered breezily. She wasn't going to waste a bit of energy thinking about Bill today.

Mr. Norquist blew a piercing blast on his whistle. "Line up here for the Egg Race!" he shouted. Uh-oh! thought Jamie. I'd better hurry! She ran over to the spot where she'd left the magic sneakers.

They weren't there.

Jamie spun around and searched the surrounding area.

Still no sneakers.

"Twenty seconds!" shouted Mr. Norquist.

"Are you looking for something, Jamie?" It was Miss Duni.

"Yes," said Jamie desperately. "Have you seen a pair of pink high-tops with green laces? I know I left them here."

"Oh, Jamie, I'm sorry," said Miss Duni calmly. "I didn't know whom those sneakers belonged to. So I gave Megan Stern permission to borrow them. She's wearing them now."

For a second Jamie thought she was going to faint.

"You let Megan borrow my sneakers?" she shrieked.

Miss Duni looked bewildered. "Well, yes, Jamie. I'm sorry if you're upset — but what's the problem? You're wearing another pair!"

Jamie looked down at her old blue running shoes. "I know, Miss Duni, but those pink ones — well, they're my good-luck sneakers. I can't run in the race without them!"

Randy came rushing up. "Come on, Jamie!" she gasped. "The race is just about to . . . "

There was a piercing whistle blast. "And they're off!" shouted Mr. Norquist. The race had just started.

"Megan's running with my sneakers on!" Jamie told Randy.

"Your sneakers? But she'll . . . "

"I know!" Jamie said wildly. "We've got to stop her!"

And the two girls dashed toward the starting line.

It was too late. Megan was already out on the field.

In the Egg Race, the racers had to carry hard-boiled eggs across the field on spoons. Usually the winner was the one who walked the most slowly. When people tried to run, their eggs always fell off their spoons.

But as Jamie and Randy watched, Megan ran faster and faster — and her egg never even so much as wobbled. It stayed on her spoon as if it had been glued there. The magic sneakers were turning her into a great athlete, instead of Jamie!

There were murmurs of amazement from the onlookers. "I never knew Megan had such great coordination!" said Mr. Norquist, who was standing next to Jamie. "Look at the way she's keeping that egg balanced!"

"Mr. Norquist, you've got to stop her!" Randy begged him desperately.

He looked startled. "Why on earth should I? She's winning!"

"I know, but — but she's allergic to eggs!" said Jamie. It was the best she could manage on such short notice. She couldn't tell him that Megan might disappear at any moment.

Mr. Norquist laughed. "I think she'll be okay," he said. Suddenly he stopped and stared out at the field.

"Wait! Wait, she's down!" he said tensely.

It was true. Megan was lying on the ground, clutching her ankle and crying.

"An injury! An injury!" yelled Mr. Norquist. "Everybody stand back! I'll handle this!" he thundered, making his way toward Megan.

No one stood back. Everyone rushed over to Megan except for the rest of the racers. Unsure about what to do, they stood forgotten on the field clutching their spoons.

"Does she need artificial respiration?" asked Marlene Heiklen hopefully. "I just learned it in junior lifesaving class."

"Nope. She's breathing fine. Looks like a sprain," Mr. Norquist bellowed. "We better get her to the nurse's office. Clear the way, everyone! Clear the way! We've got a medical emergency here!"

"Oh, thank heaven!" Jamie breathed to Randy. "Now I'll be able to get my sneakers back!"

"Why, Jamie Keenan, I'm shocked by your unfeeling attitude! Thinking about your sneakers when your classmate is hurt!" said Miss Duni.

"Oh, I'm thinking about Megan, too!" Jamie told her earnestly. "Believe me, I am! I — I just want the sneakers back for the rest of the races."

"Jamie, how many times do I have to say it? Events like Field Day are not the reason we come to school! We come here to study and get an education! Besides, you'd better let the nurse take the sneakers off. She may need to cut them off if Megan's ankle is too swollen."

"*Cut them off*!" Jamie and Randy cried in unison. What would happen to the sneakers' magic if they were sliced up?

"Clear the way, everyone!" shouted Mr. Norquist. "We've got an injured person here!"

In a couple of minutes he was back. "The nurse is with her now," he said with satisfaction. "She'll be fine — thanks to our quick action. Okay! Let's get this show on the road again! Time for the Hurdle Relay! Keenan, you weren't in the Egg Race," he added suddenly, catching sight of Jamie. "Go get in line. You can be part of the first team."

Dragging her feet in her useless blue running shoes, Jamie walked slowly over to the starting line. Bill Baird uttered a big, theatrical groan when he saw her.

"Oh, no! Are you on our team?" he said. "We might as well give up right now. Miss Klutz will be sure to lose the race for us."

"Shut up, Bill," said Randy halfheartedly. "It doesn't matter, Jamie," she added. "We don't have to win. Let's just have fun. Right, team?"

The rest of the kids on the team looked away. Oh, no! Jamie thought. They all expected her to lose!

The rest of the teams were lining up. Starr Stuart was on the team next to Jamie's. Calmly she refastened her ponytail and did a few professional-looking stretches.

Don't worry, Jamie tried to tell herself. Remember, you got Starr to believe that Elvis was in her living room. But somehow that thought didn't cheer Jamie up any.

"Let's see, team," said Randy brightly. "Who should go first?"

"Klutz-brain," said Bill immediately. "Let's get her out of the way. Maybe we can make up the difference when she's finished."

There was no argument from the rest of Jamie's teammates. Randy gave her a comforting pat on the shoulder, but didn't say anything. Even she knows I'm going to wreck it for all of us, Jamie thought sadly.

"Take your places!" called Mr. Norquist. Slowly Jamie positioned herself at the starting line. A large lump formed in her throat.

"On your mark!" shouted Mr. Dooley.

"There's a fruit fly in your hair," Bill Baird jeered.

"Get set!"

Jamie counted the six hurdles ahead of her. They looked more treacherous than Mount Everest. "Don't worry, Jamie," Randy whispered.

"*Go!*"

Jamie was off.

Suddenly it didn't seem to matter anymore. This is just a race, Jamie told herself. Even if I trip over every hurdle and no one ever speaks to me again and I never make any friends again and I break both legs and never walk again and my family disowns me and I starve to death, it's still just a . . .

Jamie cleared the first hurdle before she even thought about what she was doing.

Hey! she thought, totally astonished. I did it!

She looked backward for a fraction of a second, unable to believe she hadn't knocked it over.

"Go, Jamie!" called Miss Duni. "Fly like a bee!"

Jamie flung herself over the second hurdle. In the lane next to her, Starr Stuart stumbled and fell onto her face. "Oof!" she grunted as her hurdle toppled over onto her.

Jamie kept going. Don't look back anymore, she told herself breathlessly. You'll lose time that way.

Third hurdle. Fourth. A flash of the faces on the sidelines shouting encouragement.

I can't believe this! thought Jamie. Behind her, in another lane, she heard a thudding sound. Someone had knocked over another hurdle.

Fifth. Jamie's breath was ragged in her throat, and her legs were starting to ache. Just try to get over one more, she begged herself. Just one more . . .

"Go, Jamie!" she heard Randy screaming.

Here came the sixth hurdle. Jamie gathered up all her strength and flung herself over it.

She was over. Without stopping to think about what she'd just done, Jamie pelted across the finish line and handed the baton to the next person on her team. Instantly Bill Baird set off.

"You did it!" Randy screamed, giving Jamie a suffocating hug.

"I — I did?" Jamie stammered.

For the first time she turned and stared at the field. Randy was right. Somehow Jamie had managed to beat all her opponents. And she'd done it without her magic sneakers!

Jamie realized that her mouth was open in shock. She closed it. Then she opened it again.

"Do you — do you think the magic somehow soaked into my feet from wearing the sneakers so much?" she asked in a stunned voice.

Randy smiled at her fondly. "Nope. I think the *practicing* was the magic, Jamie. Look how hard you worked all week! You did it all by yourself," she finished. "Without the help of your high-tops."

"I guess you're right," said Jamie.

I did it all by myself, she thought. I practiced and practiced, and I stopped being a klutz. It didn't take magic — just hard work.

This must be the way *real* athletes feel, she thought triumphantly. No wonder they win!

Chapter Twelve

"I guess you're a competitor after all, Keenan,"
said Mr. Norquist. He shook his head in amazement. "I've never seen such an improvement in
a basically clumsy kid — I mean, in a student
who didn't want to go the distance. I'll have to
get you onto one of the school teams."

It was amazing. Jamie's team won because of
the head start she'd given them. Then she and
Randy went on to win the Sack Race. Then Jamie
didn't win the hundred yard dash — but she did
come in fourth. And for someone who'd never
before managed to complete a race without falling on her face, that was pretty spectacular.

Starr Stuart came up to Jamie after the hundred yard dash. "Congratulations," she said.
"You're doing great! Oh, and that reminds me —
what did you mean about Elvis the other day?"

Jamie regarded her blankly. "I don't know," she
said. "I just somehow felt like saying his name
when you went by. Do you think I'm psychic or
something?"

Starr shuddered. "I hope not. Anyway, congratulations."

111

Jamie grinned as Starr walked off. I'm going to have to be careful not to get a swelled head, what with all these celebrities congratulating me, she thought.

It was almost as satisfying as winning to see Bill Baird lose race after race. She especially enjoyed watching him run the Mini-Marathon.

Bill swaggered up to the starting line and rubbed his hands. "I'm going to eat up the miles," he told Miss Duni proudly. She and Jamie were standing on the sidelines watching the racers preparing to start. "You know, I've been in three Iron Man triathlons," he went on.

"What are those, dear?" Miss Duni asked. "Something you do with your toy soldiers?"

"No!" Billy answered indignantly. "They're the toughest kind of race in the history of the world, I bet. The kind where you have to run a *real* marathon plus swim three miles. Then you finish it off with a fifty-mile bike ride."

"Oh, my!" Miss Duni said politely. "I could never do that!"

"No, probably not," Bill said. "It takes a lot of training." He glanced over at Mike Liu, who was standing next to him at the starting line. "Liu here will probably start getting cramps about three steps into the thing."

Actually, Mike Liu did fine. It was Bill who had the trouble. Halfway through the first circuit around the school, he began clutching his side

112

and breathing hard. Jamie, who was still watching from the sidelines, threw a cup of water in his face as he went by.

"I've seen spectators do that to *real* marathoners," she called after him.

Next, Bill got a blister on his left heel. He still wouldn't quit, though — Jamie had to admire him for that. He simply stopped running and started lurching instead.

By the time the race had shifted over to the track, Bill looked like a creature from another planet. A *tortured* creature from another planet. He was hobbling and sweating and gasping and muttering angrily to himself.

"Child abuse!" Jamie and Randy heard him say. "Going to tell my father!"

And when he came in last, he was still complaining. "You should know better than to put healthy children through this kind of thing!" he croaked at Mr. Norquist in front of everyone. "I'm telling my parents! You tortured us for your own amusement!"

"Baird, it doesn't exactly amuse me to see someone in bad shape, like you," said Mr. Norquist. "Besides, everyone else in the race seems to have managed okay. Mike Liu looks fine." Mike had won the race.

Bill was still furious. "I'm going to the nurse's office," he said. "Someone needs to make sure I'm okay."

"The nurse!" Jamie gasped. "Megan's down there! I forgot all about her! I've got to see what happened! Mr. Norquist, may I please go see Megan?"

"Don't you want to get your medals?" asked Mr. Norquist. "We're just about to have the awards ceremony. The band just got here to play while everybody marches up." He pointed across the field to three third-graders holding trumpets. They were trying to rehearse some marching music, but it sounded more like a contest to see whose trumpet could squawk loudest.

"Could you save my medals for me?" asked Jamie. "I'm sure Megan would love to hear about the races. She's probably pretty lonely down there."

"Okay, Keenan," said Mr. Norquist. He gave her a friendly slap on the back. "You did a nice job today."

"You really look fine to me," the nurse, Mrs. Randol telling Bill the Pill when Jamie got to her office. "I'll give you a bandage for your heel, but other than that you're okay."

"Okay!" yelled Bill furiously. "What kind of nurse are you? Can't you see I've got all kinds of problems?"

"Yes, I can see that," said Mrs. Randolph coolly, "but none of them are physical. See you later, Bill."

114

As Bill stormed out, Mrs. Randolph turned to Jamie. "What can I do for you, dear?"

"I — I was wondering how Megan's doing," Jamie faltered. "Um, where *is* Megan?" There were three beds in the nurse's office, but Megan was nowhere to be seen.

"Oh, she's in the little back room," said Mrs. Randolph. "I put her in there because I thought it would be quieter." She stood and walked to the door of the back room. "Let's go and see how she's doing. Why, Megan, what's the matter?"

Jamie tiptoed up behind her and peeked into the back room. Megan was crying!

"I — I fell asleep," Megan sobbed. Jamie saw that she was still wearing the sneakers. "And when I woke up, I wasn't there! I mean, I was invisible! I could feel myself lying on the bed, but I couldn't see myself! Oh, Mrs. Randolph, it was awful!"

"There, there, dear," Mrs. Randolph soothed her. "You must have bumped your head when you fell."

"But I didn't!" Megan said. "I didn't even hurt my ankle that badly! I was perfectly fine when Mr. Norquist brought me here."

Mrs. Randolph laughed tolerantly. "Well, dear, you're certainly here now, aren't you?" she asked. "And that's all that matters." Jamie could tell she didn't believe a word Megan had said. "Here's a friend to visit you," she went on.

"Hi, Jamie!" said Megan. "How was Field Day?"

"Oh, it was okay. Megan, I was wondering if I could have my sneakers back?"

"Oh, are those yours? Sure! Thanks for lending them to me. I forgot mine this morning."

She started to unlace them, then suddenly stopped. "Oh, no, wait!" she said. "My shoes are still outside and my sneakers are in my locker! Can I give these back to you tomorrow, Jamie?"

Locker. Locker. Jamie wanted to jump into the air. On top of everything else, she'd suddenly thought of an idea for her bug project, just as she'd been hoping she would.

"You know what?" said Jamie. "I'll run out and get your shoes for you. I'm sure they'd be more comfortable for you than wearing mine. It's okay — I don't mind a bit."

Holding her sneakers tightly, Jamie rushed out of the room. I've got to hurry, she thought.

School would be out in half an hour. The awards ceremony was still going on outside — Jamie could see it through the window. If she could turn invisible right now, she'd have just enough time to do a little work on her fruit fly project. And there was one part of the project she had to do without Bill Baird seeing her.

116

Chapter Thirteen

"Well, Jamie," said Mrs. Keenan at breakfast the next morning, "are you nervous about giving your insect report today?"

"*I'm* nervous," said Margaret before Jamie could answer. "I'm afraid she's not really going to give that report. I'm afraid Bug Sessions are never going to end, and we'll hear about them forever."

"I'm fine, Mom," said Jamie with a smile. "I think my report will go very well."

Her father lowered the newspaper. "What's the point of this project?" he asked.

"It's hard to explain, Dad," said Jamie. "It's sort of about how fruit flies can survive even in dangerous conditions."

"Sounds interesting," said her father. He ducked back behind the newspaper.

"Sounds revolting," said Betsy with a shudder. "Jamie, do you have to talk about this while we're eating?"

"You're not eating," Tim pointed out. "Mom, can I have Betsy's waffles?"

"*No*, Tim," said Mrs. Keenan. "You'd better get your books and things together, Jamie. Your bus will be here in ten minutes."

"My stuff's already together, Mom," Jamie answered happily. "I got it all ready last night. I guess I'll just walk out to the bus stop and wait. Today's the big day for my big moment!"

Margaret rolled her eyes.

"That was a very interesting report, Dan," said Miss Duni. "I'm sure none of us knew that termites chewed up so many different kinds of wood. How did you collect all the sawdust you showed us?"

"Well, first I took lots of different wooden things from around the house," said Dan McCarthy. "For the pine I borrowed one of my mother's wooden spoons, and for the oak I borrowed a leg from one of our kitchen chairs, and for the chestnut I borrowed one of the floorboards in the living room. Then I just let the termites loose until there was nothing left but sawdust. That's all there was to it!"

"Well, you've done a very impressive job," said Miss Duni. "And you've certainly made it clear how destructive termites can be. Now it's Bill Baird's turn, I think. Bill, are you ready?"

Bill stood up. His arm was in a sling, and he was hunched over like a little old man. "Not quite, Miss Duni," he said in a weak, hoarse voice. "You know, all those injuries I got at Field Day yesterday kept me from putting the finishing touches on the project. It's almost ready, but I still need a couple more days."

Miss Duni stared at him for a minute. "You have one more day to come up with something," she said firmly. "And I sincerely hope it will be worth the wait. That means it's Jamie's turn. Jamie, are you ready?"

Jamie stood up. "Yes, I am," she said. "But my project's not in this room. It's down the hall, next to my locker. Could we all go out there?"

"Why, Jamie, how original!" said Miss Duni. "Of course. Okay, class. Let's get in line and walk down the hall. And I mean *walk*!"

Half the class was stampeding out the door, and the other half was already tearing down the hall toward Jamie's locker before Miss Duni had even finished her sentence.

Bill Baird limped along behind the rest of the class. "I can't walk!" Jamie heard him complaining. "I'm wounded from Field Day!" But no one paid any attention to him.

The rest of the class was already gathered around Jamie's locker when Bill finally got there. "Oh, there you are," said Jamie. "I'm glad you're here, Bill, because I need your help. Could you please unlock your locker for me?"

"Why?" Bill asked.

"Because my project is *in* your locker," said Jamie.

For a second Bill just stared at her. Then, muttering under his breath, he fiddled with his combination. He was about to open the door when Jamie stopped him.

"That's fine, Bill," she said. "I'll take it from here."

She turned to the class. "You know, you can really find out a lot by studying an insect," she said. "One of the things I learned about fruit flies is that they breed really fast. Bill and I started out with just a couple of them, and now we have hundreds in our aquarium.

"And you can also find a lot about a person by having a locker next to him," Jamie went on. "One of the things I found out about Bill was that he doesn't clean his locker out too often. There's lots of old food in there — old banana peels, apple cores, things like that."

Starr Stuart shuddered.

"Well, it seemed kind of gross to me, too," said Jamie earnestly, "but then I started to wonder. If our fruit flies did so well living in an empty aquarium, then wouldn't they do really well in a place like Bill's locker? I mean, it's filled with old food, and there's lots of space for them . . . "

Bill was glaring furiously at her. Jamie gave him an innocent smile.

"That was good thinking, Jamie," said Miss Duni. "So what did you do?"

"It was very simple," said Jamie. "Last night I collected some fruit flies and put them into a jar. Then I dipped a plastic straw into some sugar water. When the flies came up to drink the sugar water, a few of them walked inside the straw."

"When did you do all this?" Miss Duni asked in a puzzled voice. "Field Day took up so much time!"

"Oh, I just squeezed it in somehow," said Jamie vaguely. She wasn't going to tell Miss Duni that she'd done it all in the few minutes left before the Field Day awards ceremony ended. *That* was why she'd needed to get her sneakers back — so she could turn invisible fast!

"So I had this straw full of fruit flies," Jamie said. "I just took the straw and blew into it so that the flies entered Bill's locker right *here*."

She pointed to the tiny vent at the top of the locker.

"Those flies have been in there all night," she said. "And since fruit flies breed so quickly — and since there was plenty of garbage for them to eat — I'm guessing that . . . "

She reached forward and opened Bill's door with a flourish.

A cloud of fruit flies — millions and millions and millions of them — swarmed into the air and filled the hall.

"I can prove," said Jamie, "that Bill's locker is an excellent breeding ground for pests." Everyone burst out laughing.

At last Miss Duni found her voice. "Not pests, Jamie," she said. "Fruit flies are our *friends*. Okay, everyone, it's time to get back to our classroom."

"What kind of grade do you think Miss Duni will give you?" Randy whispered to Jamie as the two girls walked back.

"I don't know," said Jamie. "She did say it was a very original idea. It doesn't really matter, though. All that counts is that it's going to take a very long time for those flies to move out of Bill's locker."

"But won't the flies bother you, too?" Randy asked. "I mean, your locker is right next door to Bill's."

"Oh, Ran, I forgot to tell you — I'll be sharing your locker with you for the rest of the year."

"Listen, Jamie, my locker is neat, and I want it to stay that way. Do you really have to share it?"

"Come on, Ran, what are best friends for? Look on the bright side — if I start to get on your nerves, I can just disappear!"

If you enjoyed GETTING EVEN, you won't want to miss WACKY WEDDING, the second book in the SEE-THROUGH KID series. . . .

Jamie's cousin Marylou is getting married, and Jamie is sure she'll be asked to be the flower girl. She can't wait to get all dressed up and march down the aisle. Then she discovers that not only has Marylou chosen another flower girl, but she hasn't even invited Jamie to the wedding! That doesn't stop the See-Through Kid — with the help of her magic sneakers, Jamie decides to *sneak* into the wedding, with hilarious results.